MY HAUNTED HOME

MY HAUNTED HOME

STORIES

VICTORIA HOOD

FC2

TUSCALOOSA

FC2 is an imprint of the University of Alabama Press

Inquiries about reproducing material from this work should be addressed to the University of Alabama Press

Book Design: Publications Unit, Department of English, Illinois State University; Director: Steve Halle, Production Assistant: Qulea Anderson
Cover image: © Dmitry Lukash | Dreamstime.com
Cover design: Lou Robinson
Typeface: Bodoni 72

Library of Congress Cataloging-in-Publication Data is available from the Library of Congress.

ISBN: 978-1-57366-196-6
E-ISBN: 978-1-57366-898-9

DEDICATION
For my dead mom and alive dad

TABLE OF CONTENTS

PART I

PART II

MY HAUNTED HOME

PART I

The Teeth, the Way I Smile

Mom is trapped in the mirror. But not like bloody mary; she's trapped in my cheekbones and my almond eyes. The way that my eyes are brown, but my sister's are blue. Mom is trapped in the edges of my lips, but she frowns as I smile because that means that she isn't really dead. It means her wishes can't come true if I live.

She sleeps softly as the bathroom is dark, dark, not bright, but a hard and shy shade of darkness, blackness, a sleeping fog. She sleeps and rests, just like she wanted, but then I walk in and grab her by her ankles, pulling her out of bed. Her eyes closed, mind fading into the sweet sounds of sleep, until I bash the door in, break the windows, rip her out of bed as she cries and screams.

The light turns on, and she is awake. Her eyes tired, worn duffle bags of worn-out life pulling her face toward the ground. The light turns on, and her decaying face turns into mine—slightly less tired, plump, and full of life. Hers decaying, burning, worms eating her. Mine yawning, living, wiping the gunk from my eyes.

I can hear her begging to be set free. I see it in my eyes, not in the pupils, not in the iris, but behind them, in the socket where she screams. I can hear her in my bones telling me that she's tired, that she wants to go to bed. When I close the door, turn off the lights, I can hear her drop to the floor, exhausted and already asleep. When the lights are off, I can hear her snoring, I can hear her dreams, I can hear her dreaming.

In her dreams she is free from the mirror. She is dead like she always wanted to be. In her dreams her children are happy, her husband has moved on, her back is in alignment, no longer rubbing against itself. In her dreams we are all together, not in death or in life, but together in our favorite memories of each other. In her dreams we are not in a mirror, in a bathroom, in a house, but we are alive inside some cloud, floating above all the things we fought about. In her dreams she is alive, but in her dreams she is finally dead.

When I open the door, when I turn the lights on, I hear the military bell ring, and she stands at attention. She was once my owner, but now she lives within the mole on my cheek and my crooked teeth. She used to sing me awake, slowly opening the door and turning the lights on, but now I sound the alarm, no warning, rushing in and pulling her blanket off.

In my dreams I look like no one, I look like me, I look like a person who is happy, a person who doesn't have a dead mom, but rather a person who is a twenty-two-year-old girl. In my dreams I can tell my mom I love her, she can meet my fiancé, she can tell me she loves me. In my dreams my face is my own, I don't own a mirror, I don't see a reflection, I can't see myself. In my dreams she is happy; that is all we've ever wanted for her.

When I wake up, I look at my phone, I laugh, I hit snooze on my alarm. When I wake up, I am next to my fiancé, covered in blankets, tossing and turning. When I wake up, I am not alone trapped in a mirror but alone trapped in her body, in her face, in her compliments of beauty of her memory of the way she used to smile of the way people remembered her when she was alive and herself.

In my dreams I do not have a face or body. Perhaps I am only shape and air. In her dreams she is also this. We are melding together through our wishes to end our haunting, to become two, to separate and hide in our own corners, but even then, we are melting into the same shapeless frame of thoughts she gave me—tainted, poisoned, never my own.

When I wake up, I go to the bathroom and I turn on the lights and I summon Mom who wishes she was not her, but maybe bloody mary, and Mom could run away, could attack me, could perform a ritual to get out. Turn around three times in a circle and chant that I wish my mom wasn't dead, I wish my mom didn't kill herself, I wish my mom looked like my sister. When I wake up, I wake her up so then we can suffer together.

My mom is trapped in the mirror, in the bathroom, in my apartment, at my school, in the public restrooms, and in the dark reflection of my phone, in the camera, in my photos. My mom is trapped in the way my eyes squint when I smile so when I get married all they will see is her, wishing she was there, wishing I could have her there. My mom is trapped in my height, trapped in my knees, trapped in my bad back. My mom is trapped in the mirror but is living inside of me feasting on my life, wishing she could have hers back. My mom is trapped in my heart wishing I could forget, forgive, move on, and stop writing stories about her so she could just die already.

I Like It

I like to bite the skin on my hands. To pull and teethe and grip and bite. To eat through to the bone until it can be licked clean—no more veins or skin or nail.

I like to bite the skin on my fingers. To skin them. To fillet. To eat and satiate. To eat through until the sounds are gone.

I like to drown out my mom. To bite and nibble even when she says stop. Stop. No, keep going. Keep eating and gnawing until the blood runs out and dries inside my stomach.

I like the outside to be inside. To unzip and button it up differently. Sewing it together in a different area. New puzzle. Rearranging and reentering. No need for knocking because I can let myself in.

I like to knock down the door and burst in. I like to eat, but only myself. The rest of the world is tainted and poisoned, but my skin is blessed and fluid. Delicious.

I like the thickness of my skin. The durability and longevity. The lovely resistance of my teeth trying to chomp, trying to become one, trying to eat and enjoy and munch.

I wonder what will happen when it's all bone. When my skeleton becomes my skin and my hands fall off. I like to think about that. To wish and plan for it.

I like to eat and eat and eat my hands as a snack. It's not really a meal, but something to tide me over. To sate my mouth and my lust and my hunger until it is time to move on.

I don't like to bite my nails. They're stale and narrow. I like the meat, the flesh, the living, the squirm, the blood. I like to make it dead, but alive inside of me.

I like to picture these things even when I can't bite and chew and eat. When there are too many people around and watching and I must only look and dream of my meaty hands.

I like the pain and agony of the biting. I like the sound of my teeth clashing into each other. Battling for the next bite. For the next taste. The skin evaporating and fading into my tongue. My tongue taking over and pushing it into my throat.

I like the travel. Following my skin and my meat down my throat into my guts. Into my organs. I like to follow it. It makes me smile.

I like when the thinking stops and the habit kicks in. I like when the thoughts leave and all that happens is the collapse of skin, oozing blood, metal taste, and chunks disappearing. I like when it envelops me.

I wonder how many bites it will take to get to my center. I wonder how much needs to leave and how many times I'll be told to stop. I guess I can only find out.

I like to find out. I like to fill my mouth with myself until myself is only in me. I'm excited to keep eating. I like it.

My Rain Monster

There is some sort of rain monster that lives in my kitchen. Some days I walk in, and it is all wet and mushy. Other days it is dry and heavy. On special occasions, I come home and see my rain monster just starting, or ending, or strictly in the middle.

It doesn't bother me much; I am familiar with the need to do your job and leave. Sometimes it feels useless: I don't have any crops, I don't own a cow, it is just a kitchen in suburbia. Then I remember that everyone hates their jobs anyway because someone always thinks it's useless.

Sometimes I will leave thank-you notes so my rain monster knows that someone appreciates them. I always find them soggy and unopened, but I know they mean something. Sometimes I find lemon peels on the ground, which means they must be eating my lemons, but I don't mind. I do not like lemons very much anyway.

I think they started about four months ago, and it seems to only be a part-time job. I think it must be a government job because of the loathing and also the benefits. I am sure they get a bonus if they can soak through my floor within the year.

I don't clean up my kitchen. I just let it evaporate naturally. I feel as though if I clean it then it wins, and I lose. I think that since I am a taxpayer, I would get a say in the wetness of my kitchen but not today—or for the past four months.

They usually come Tuesday-Thursday every week. My favorite times are when they come at night because sometimes they will curl up in bed with me when they're done and rub their wet pruny hands over my back. I like the sound of their prunes on my soft bed. Sometimes I wet the bed, and I'm not sure if it's their soak or my pee.

I thought about asking them to leave when it first started, but I felt rude intruding on their job. They're just trying to make a living the same as the rest of us. They look just like us too, a frown and eyebrows and sometimes they cry. Or maybe it's just the rain running down their face. Either way, it is mesmerizing.

I want to be in love with the rain monster, but then they'll never come back. It'll only create more chaos and more wetness. Sometimes I wish I could help them, take away their stick and sad cloud and poke at it so they could take a break. I wish they could be in love with me.

Sometimes I ask it questions, and it ignores me, which only inflames my love more. Longing for their long, wet hair to tuck me in at night. Sometimes I wish I could sleep within them, cut them open and sleep in their thick, red sauce.

This is why I know I can't be in love. I am too young. Too dry.

The Election

The ghosts have informed me that I need to redecorate.

I think the biggest mistake I made was listening to them. They never agree, they make horrible choices, and I hate the color yellow. It always seems that decorators only redecorate for the money and never for the love.

These ghosts of mine that I never invited have become noisier than I had wanted. They made a committee, they rearranged, and they only invited me once the decisions were made.

Rachel is a secret misogynist and most likely a racist. She wants everything to scream at you when you come in, but I do not have the budget for such investments.

Brianna is a lesbian, which means Rachel does not like her, but I connect most closely to Brianna. She wants things to be a stormy grey but also to have rain clouds. I do not like rain.

Fiona is too happy to exist in this household. Her resentment level for her age is terribly low, and she smells bad. Also, she likes to bedazzle. Jack is sensible but too minimalistic. He wants me to spark joy, but I tell him no. He doesn't like being told what to do. Neither do I. I wish that for the sake of my house and the things that live inside it, I did not need to listen to them. I wish I could move out and on, but I cannot because I've saved no money since I moved in. The rest of the ghosts do not control a high enough stock to get a vote. These ghosts I have listed campaigned for their voices, and yet their voices suck. It seems that it is always the loudest ghosts that are also the most annoying. Though the ghost that tickles my feet at night is not my favorite either. I try to change the subject when they make recommendations, but they never fall for it. I try to inform them that this is my house, but they inform me I'd have to die first. I don't think I'm ready for that.

Sometimes I think about what it would be like to join in the ghostly nights and the elections they hold without me there. I wonder how I would fit into their society—if I would be a Rachel or a Brianna or a Fiona or a Jack. I wonder if it would be possible even to be myself, but that is never an option on the quiz.

I try not to pick favorites, but it becomes obvious after I paint the walls. Truthfully, I think I have a crush on Brianna and I'm trying to impress her. I've never dated a ghost, but transparency is good in a relationship. I am just not ready to import rain clouds yet.

At night, Jack tries to crawl into my bed. I pretend to sleep, and he rustles my covers. I tell him to go away, and sometimes he listens. He doesn't do anything. He just likes to cuddle, but I need personal space. I tell him this. Rachel takes his side.

The only ghost I never feel close enough to is Fiona because her happiness hangs over the house like oil over water. They never meld together, and the tension is always strong.

During the day I work from home. I started a business where I sell slightly haunted goods to faux goths online. It is not hard to trick them, and it has become entirely too easy to ensure they are haunted. I have begun putting the ghost babies of Rachel and Jack into these goods. Ghost babies don't grow. They just whine and fall over. That is all these goods do. The faux goths love it. I only have one one-star review from a real goth who knows I only sell baby ghosts, but he has been outvoted.

Every Wednesday we have family dinner. All thirty-seven ghosts are invited, but only the five of us sit at the table. Everyone else lines up buffet style, gets their food, and sits crisscross applesauce in front of us. I think they place bets on these dinners. I'm sure I never win.

There is always a debate that I am not prepared for on Wednesdays. Usually, it is on how humans and ghosts could never live together. Sometimes the debate is over when the rain clouds will be imported. It almost always results in someone crying. Can't the tears be the rain? Brianna never agrees to this. She tells me there is a distinct difference, and I just have to trust her.

At dinner we discuss the decorating plan for the week. Ultimately, I decide what happens since I'm the one with the credit card, but usually this dinner lasts for seven hours, minimum. There is yelling and booing and crying. Most of which comes from me, some of which comes from Fiona. She isn't strong enough for a ghostly life.

This week I inform them that we have elections coming up. No one remembers this fact. I tell them they should have been campaigning for the last seven months. Everyone is shocked. I have been working on my campaign for the last eight; now I know why no one has taken the time to come to my meetings. It is time for change, and we all need to remember that life is short: we need to campaign for our beliefs. No one laughs even though I tell them it was supposed to be a joke. I explain that it is funny, because they are all dead. They do not think it is funny. I still do.

At night I hear the flyers go up and the ghosts conspiring. I wonder who will win. No one has ever beaten an incumbent, but I also hope for a fresh face, maybe someone who smells better. On Friday we hold the vote. All thirty-seven ghosts line up and vote. Each ghost seems to take an hour to decide, and the election takes so long that it spans across three days. I wait for the news, the fresh news and new faces.

The results are in.

I'm out.

This is an outrage! I'm the one who pays rent. They tell me that they have voted Brianna as the head of household. I tell them a human must be the head of household. They tell me that I can ask for a recount, but I got no votes. All I can do is cry because I'm the only one who even tried to campaign. You should have come to my meetings, I tell them.

On Saturday I am instructed to kill myself. To sacrifice my body so that Brianna can inhabit it. I am happy that if anyone is to own my body that it is Brianna. I follow their instructions. Maybe now she will be able to love me like I have loved her.

On Sunday Brianna has become me.

On Monday she moves out.

My Lazy Eye

There is a demon living in my eye. The hole of my eye, but not exactly my whole eye. It does not control me, doesn't even control my eye, but moves it around, lets it peek around the corner. Sometimes people will notice it and ask if that is my lazy eye, but it is not a lazy eye: it is just my demon eye.

I don't see things differently out of my demon eye. I'm not sure why the demon has chosen that eye—I don't know what is so special about it. I'm not sure what he sees, what he gets out of this deal, but I do not complain. It's nice to have a friend.

We do not talk, this demon and myself. He may not even call me his friend, but in this body I find us to click, to be a clique, to talk of clicks and chicks and dicks and all the things friends gossip about. I dream to know about his wife, his daughter. I would tell him about my dad and my sister. I vent about my dumb boyfriend and his dumb parents; he tells me that every dumb boyfriend has dumb parents. Maybe we even fall in love, me and the demon that lives in my eye. He hasn't been home in a while—he's been living in my eye. His wife gets jealous—my boyfriend says I seem distant. I seem distant because I'm falling in love with the demon inside my eye. My boyfriend breaks up with me, complains about my lazy eye. I tell him that it's not a lazy eye; it's my demon eye, but he does not understand. He'll tell his dumb parents that I'm crazy, and his parents will believe him because they're just as dumb as he always was. They can't see this little demon that lives behind my eye; I don't think he ever really got to know me. His wife will ask for a divorce, she'll take the kid, we don't mind because we want to live in our honeymoon. We get married on a yacht, but we can't get married because no one will marry me to the demon they can't see living in my eye, so we just agree that we're married. We don't want kids—we only want each other living in our home, he in the home within our home. When I cry, he can grab it and stop it from falling. No one will see my weakness anymore. I dream that one day we are fighting about taxes, he refuses to get a job, I call him lazy, he calls me dumb, he tells me I have a lazy eye even though he knows it's a demon eye. I cry, but he does not catch my tear. That is how I know it is over. I don't bother plucking him out of my eye; he will move out on his own.

I know that I am dreaming this, but I start to cry because I know it is all inevitable, but I want to love the demon living in my eye. I don't want things to end like this. I stare in the mirror, hoping he will catch my tears like I always dreamt of, but I see him crying too. He must be thinking of me. He must be dreaming my dreams and feeling my feelings. Or maybe he has a demon in his eye that he's hiding. He is so selfish: this is why he won't get a job because he's too busy worrying about the demon in his eye. I knew it would end like this: his lies, his hypocrisy, his own lazy eye. So I pluck him out, I tear at him, but he holds on, he won't let go—how would he explain that to the demon in his eye? I tear and claw and scratch and yell until there is no more eye for him to hide in.

Ants

The windowsills are full of air. They're full of dirt and ants too. I'm not sure how the ants keep marching from windowsill to windowsill, but they do. They never touch the ground, they never fly across the air, they just appear. There must be an underground tunnel somewhere.

The dirt and the ants must have come before the crumbles of cookie and life that I left there. Unless, of course, they waited to come until after. I fear that they are the only real that this house has left inside of it. I fear that I am only air and tunnels.

I watch the ants as they crawl and I watch as they apparate. There must be an underground tunnel leading from my window to the world and the world back to my window, but the walls are still intact. The floorboards haven't broken, and I don't hear the wind. I don't feel the wind on my face, on my hands; I couldn't spit on my finger and tell which direction it's blowing. I watch and wonder if they are tunneling through me, being me, becoming a part of me until they reappear— disgusted with being me.

I never disliked ants because they never did anything to me. They never told me to trust them and broke their promises. They've never told me anything. Sometimes when I see them, I wish that me and them and all our legs could create a world in which we don't need to fear a lack of legs anymore, but then I remember that wouldn't be the same. If we put all of us together, then none of us would be alive, and all our extra legs would be pointless. Besides, they wouldn't let me be an ant. Most likely because I wish I were. Too much yearning churns me out. I don't understand then why they keep me company. Do they wish too that I could leave them more food and turn my house into their underground home? Dismantling their railroad.

All signs point to this railroad, but I can't find it. That must mean there are signs that I'm missing. Signs that fell down but the government couldn't afford to put back up. No stop sign, keep driving: kill a kid and drive off. But these kids are ants, and they're driving, recklessly, from window to window.

My windows have sills, but they are so tiny. They can only hold a rock or two until they fall apart. I'm not sure how this many ants fit there. I'm not sure how many they expect to come. I was not invited to this party, I did not RSVP, I do not want to host it.

I want to kill them. To offer rejection as a lack of affirmation. I want to set them all on fire as they scream and run like ants do. But where would they go? They don't have their railroad; they only have the windows, and if they burn down my window, then they'll burn me down with it.

I'm scared of them. They're going to consume me, eventually. They're going to leave the windows, enter my bed, enter my body, create an anthill out of my organs, and crown me their queen.

I should do it, I know it. I should burn them, eat them, pile them on a piece of toast, and devour them. But I can't. The wind is too strong, and I can't seem to reach the window. I can't seem to find my way to their home to bury them alive.

Instead I'll have to open the windows and blow them out. I'll huff and I'll puff until I blow my house down: then they'll have to find a new hole. They'll have to get on their train and find somewhere else to live.

But I can't. Not yet. Their wind is stronger than mine, and I'm so scared they'll bite. Or worse, I cough one up, chew one, and create an appetite for ants. An appetite for small, innocent creatures that crawl. What a shame.

This Corner, My Corner

I've walked myself into this corner. I'm afraid I can't turn around. I was just looking for my friends.

There seems to be a distance between me and the world behind me. A world that I thought existed in peace. A world I thought we were all in together. We are not in it together because the monsters have taken control of my house, of me.

There is no noise behind me, only white blankness, empty solitude. At least in this corner there is a wall. There are two walls. There is freedom from vacancy because I am occupying this corner. This corner I can see and feel. I can see two lanes merging to become one. I can see the off-white walls meeting in their pointed crevice. I can feel the smooth walls, soft bumps becoming more real as I massage them. Nothing can belong here besides me.

I only stay at hotels with no vacancies. I sneak into rooms and hide under the bed. I only like to occupy what is already occupied. I just want to join what is already made.

The lack of beings opens the world for the monsters to hide. If we could all move into a commune together, could be together, could finally have this peace together, there would be no more room for you, or them. There would be no blank walls or high ceilings. Only us, together.

I am waiting for someone to find me. I am waiting for someone to turn me inside-right again because all my wrongs, all my insides, all of me is on the outside, and it hurts to flip the skin flip the lid flip me back around so that I'm not in this corner anymore. I don't want to miss the smooth skin of this corner, I don't want to long for the comfort occupied solitude brings me. I don't want to be alone.

I've walked myself into this corner; I put myself in time out. Maybe it was a break from all the empty jars and cookie canisters that are cluttering my kitchen. It is not my kitchen but the kitchen of someone who owns this occupied house on this occupied street. The kitchen of someone who went on vacation without telling me. I am trapped here. I wish I wasn't home alone.

Time Is Human Made

Time in the kitchen moves more slowly. Some say it's just the clocks; it's just that I wasn't quick enough to line them up, but I know it's a different universe. The time ticks away at the rate it agreed upon with something I do not know, but it always gives me mixed signals. I do not trust the kitchen. No one does.

The time in my bedroom is the fastest. The time I sleep doesn't seem to exist. I close my eyes and the alarms go off, the sun rises, the day starts moving. Please slow down, I ask it, but the time is moving too fast to listen. Let's go, let's get started, let's keep the clocks moving, it tells me. I am so dizzy.

The living room lags. It seems to drift off in the middle of a sentence. It mumbles. It eats the words without knowing where they were supposed to lead. There are decaying bodies littered on the floor.

If I'm not careful I might end up there too. Thrown out on the floor, too tired to crawl, unable to chew, stuck in the tarpit that we are supposed to live in.

My bathroom moves at normal speed. You cannot hurry a shit, you cannot slow down your piss. These are the facts we must accept. The office is zoomed in. The speed is only seen through a fish-eye lens. It makes my stomach hurt, it makes my eyes hazy. I can't seem to breathe in there, but there is so much work to get done. There are piles of it on my desk. The paper has dust, the bugs are dying, mold and moss are beginning to eat away at my belongings. I want so badly to want to be productive, but I cannot see in there anymore.

Sometimes I think I should move my office to the kitchen, but then it would become my office, and I don't need to slow down a zoomed-in room. If I could work in the kitchen, I would have all the time in the world. Maybe, I could work in my bedroom. I could time travel to a time when I am done working and I can relax. I could be productive without even trying.

My food is always older than I think, rotting and rotting in the time machine of my kitchen. The grocery store must be on a realistic timeline, thinking that food can last in a house with clocks, but my fridge has no concerns for that. Start your own farm to grow your own food, they say. However, I don't know who the people who say that are, so I don't. Trust us, they say, but I do not, cannot, won't.

Sex is never enjoyable. There is no speed that feels right. Even within the bathroom the time feels wrong. I try to watch porn to see what I'm doing wrong, but none of the people in these movies have bedrooms that move like mine. No one seems to know what to do when the time in your bedroom means they cum as soon as they enter. No one has fun in there. Move into your bathroom, they say. Please stop talking to me; I don't know how you found me, I tell them. Trust us, they say. I can't, I don't.

My TV is broken because in the future of my bedroom it is obsolete. My technologies never work anymore; the timelines don't match up. There are movie stars I've never heard of. These people weren't born yet in the world of my kitchen. I never get useful information, they never reveal lottery numbers or who to save. They only tell me gossip of a century I will never truly live in.

Inside my living room I see my hopes and dreams stuck in the tarpit of my floor. They're only metaphorical; don't name the dead bodies, they tell me. They came with their names, I tell them. No, they didn't, they tell me. Oh, what do you know, I tell them, I don't trust you, I won't trust you, I yell. I start running from the living room, but it doesn't move very fast. My feet are sticky.

I have to pee. I always have to pee. If my bladder moved any slower or any faster, I think it would be unreal. You shouldn't find relief unless the timing is correct.

We love to watch you pee, they tell me. This time I ignore them, I'm sure that they are not meant to be here, they're not meant to be talking to me. We know you're ignoring us, they tell me. God? I ask them. Don't be so dumb, they tell me.

In the office I attempt to find a new job that lets me not work from home, but I can't read any of the listings. I just want to leave, I yell at my computer. You should move out, they tell me. I want to, I tell them. Then leave, they say. I can't. Whenever I reach the door, I always forget that this isn't my home.

In the kitchen I attempt to get lunch, but my sandwich is rotten. I didn't notice until it was assembled and inside me. You should have known, they tell me. You're going to rot in here too, they tell me. I don't trust you, I tell them, you don't know me. But now the tar has eaten the kitchen. The time is moving too slowly for me to peel myself away. I am going to rot in here. You should have listened to us, they tell me.

Moving Out

I have finally finished unpacking. I'm moving out in a week but wanted to see what my home could have been if I ever gave it a chance. I threw out the boxes, unpacked the bins, painted the walls a shade of grey blue, organized my books by color and my movies by smell. It is starting to come together. It is starting to feel like I have set up shop somewhere that feels like me. I went out to get flowers: peonies. I even got fresh fruit and laid it in my new banana hanger and bowl combo. I refrigerated water. I made homemade ice cream. I baked cookies so the house would fill with the smell. I hung pictures of me laughing and removed the ones of me crying. I hung pictures of my dead mom when she was alive and my alive dad before he felt dead. I hung pictures of people I'm no longer friends with and I put on the engagement ring my ex-fiancé gave me. I lit a candle that smells like vanilla and I read a two-hundred-page book in an hour. I am breathing and I can feel the air filling and leaving me.

I've decided to have a party to commemorate what my apartment could have been if I ever cared enough when I lived here. I call my friends, the ones who aren't in any pictures; I tell them I know it is last minute, but it would mean a lot. All of them come. When they walk in, they admire my handiwork. They breathe just like I had and they can feel the air. I ask if they would prefer white or red wine, and they all say red, which is why I only bought red. At midnight we toast to my once-upon-a-time home with champagne that I bought for the occasion. They tell me I should start a business and I begin to blush.

We all become somewhat drunk, and my friend spills on my carpet. They begin to cry, and I assure them it's okay; I'm moving out. They dry the stain with their tears and they dry their face with more wine. A home that I'm leaving is a home I can feel at home with. They all laugh, but I'm sure none of them understands. None of my friends are that smart; that is why I've kept them. If I am not the smartest, I begin to think too much and I do not become myself but rather a horse that is too hungry, and nothing goes right.

At two a.m. people ask what I will do with all of this. I tell them I will leave it. I do not need to take anything with me. I will only bring my wallet and shoes. They ask if they could have the flowers, if they could take an orange for the road, if I wouldn't mind them tearing up the hardwood, if I could part with the drywall. Yes, yes, yes yes yes. Take it all, I tell them.

At three a.m. the construction workers have arrived, and demolition begins. The bricks are sawed in half so each person can carry it with them like a friendship necklace. The toilet is sold for its porcelain, and the shower curtain becomes a dress. My friends take down all my mirrors and line up enough cocaine to get us through the project. The pictures of my friends have been cut and torn and turned into papier-mâché; it is a work of art. Someone has already taken my shower tiles and my bathroom floor.

At four a.m. everyone tries my clothes on. Who will fit what? Who wore it best? Who called dibs? Who called shotgun? My lingerie looks like someone has died in it, and no one likes it. I tell them it's sexy, I try it on, and everyone thinks it looks bad.

At five a.m. the orgy begins. I do not think it was the lingerie that did it; I think it was the paint thinner from my cabinets that we all huffed. I lose track of my shins and the chins and the lumps of everyone. I am not sure if anyone is a boy or a girl or if a raccoon has snuck in at some point. At one point I thought I heard someone give birth, but I think that may have been me screaming. By the end, my windows are broken, everyone is bloody, and someone has broken my arm.

At six a.m. everyone starts to leave. They all tell me they had a lot of fun. They wish that I could move more often. My home looks like it did before I decided to move out. It is dilapidated; it looks like a home that has been foregone. It smells like chicken, even though I am a vegetarian and the aura is completely wrong.

At seven a.m. I hear my landlord pull into the driveway with those who are to move in after me. Through the window I can hear their laughs; I see their smiles that look like each of their teeth has gone to college. I crawl into the floorboards and nail them together. I close my eyes.

The Tippity Toppity

My bones are rattling around inside of my house but outside of my skin. The ghosts have turned the shower off—they must have heard my body fall apart. I'm Pinocchio, and they are the villains no one remembers. They're not turning me into a donkey, they're just stealing my wooden appendages. They are going to steal my ulna, which is my favorite bone. I wonder if my ulna will ever remember it was mine and not that stupid, wet ghost's.

My mind is haunted by vacancy. Infected by little bugs and worms. There are dead bodies molding up there in my tippity toppity. The attic of my house is the attic of my brain—I'm too scared to go into either one. I think blinking stops people from being people. Every time we blink we become dogs, cats, worms, logs, but then we blink again and we are us.

They took it. They took my ulna and my femur and my patella. Now we are all just naked bones because they tried my skin on and stretched it out. Skin is like pants: when you're wet they don't go on, but they wouldn't stop. My mind is infested with termites that are eating away at the wood of my body. The structure is becoming loose. The bolts are shaking from the weight of my body, the weight of all the couches and chairs that live inside of me. My attic has water damage from the wet, dripping ghosts that are infesting my house. I clean up after them. They're always in the shower, always trying to get clean, be cleaner, but every time they shower, their skin molts off of their bones, and they just become creaky skeletons. I don't know where they keep getting more skin.

My wooden body is going to get soggy. They took my bones and drowned the termites; now all I have are their porcelain bones, at least the ones they left.

I reassemble myself, and once my tippity toppity is back, I look in the mirror, but I am wet. I am soaking wet, and my bones are bloating like those river bodies. Those ghosts made me fat. They soaked my bones in fat until I looked like them—no wonder my skin didn't fit on them.

The wind blows my body down, and I'm scattered across my bedroom. My legs and my knees are somewhere else; they ran off, my legs have become someone else; they ran off, my attic is being demolished by those sopping wet ghosts, and I can't defend it.

They call to me, those ghosts. They're in the shower cleaning their new bones and they want me to join. I'm not a ghost, I tell them, but they don't have voices because they're just lousy ghosts. They cheer me on; they beg me to come. I'm not a ghost, I yell at them. I take one of my phalanges and throw it at them. They catch it with their mouths and eat it, but they have no organs, so it just falls to the ground.

I go to the shower to collect my body; I try to pick up my phalange, but they pull me in, they hold me under, trying to drown my skeleton, but without my skin I'm just rattling bones so it does nothing to me. My mind is haunted by the vacancy of fog, the openness of walls in an empty room. My mind has become a window, not a wall. Not a television, only a remote, always changing.

I've decided that I hate the shower, it's too hot. I turn it off, and the wet ghosts get angry and try to take my patella, but they're stupid ghosts and miss. I take their patella and eat it, but I don't have a stomach anymore so it just falls to the ground. I stick my tongue out at them, but I don't have one anymore so I stick my finger through my mouth hole and wave it at them. They think that we're friends. I tell them I wouldn't be friends with ghosts because I'm not a ghost.

They stick their fingers through their mouth holes and wave them at me.

The Contents of My Heart, My Stomach

My fridge is haunted by me.

    My fridge is haunted by the ten-year-old girl who doesn't like her
    food touching.

My fridge is contaminated by the food that lies on the shelf,

        being itself, showing its skin, the feathers, the beak.

    My fridge is haunted by a sixteen-year-old who doesn't want her
    food to touch,

      won't eat anything when anyone can see her,

      refuses to let the noodles touch the broccoli, not on her plate,

      not in her mouth, don't touch, don't touch.

My fridge is haunted by the dead body that I lug around.

    My fridge is haunted by the vampire who sucks my blood.

I roast the potatoes, covered in blood, and return them to my fridge for the vampire to suck on.

My fridge is haunted by a crying baby who won't shut the fuck up.
The milk is too old to give them, it has already curdled into cheese.
The formula is not formula, but it has also curdled into cheese.
The vampire won't eat it, nobody will eat it, because it won't stop crying.

My fridge is haunted by my fingers, fingernails, fingerprints.
They won't wipe off; they contaminate the contaminants.

My fridge is hiding in the corner, hiding from me so that I won't yell at it.

My fridge is haunted by the melted ice cubes turned into water, becoming stale.
My fridge is haunted by the carrots that act as if they are real.
My fridge is haunted by my memories of cake.
My fridge is haunted by a ghost of someone who knew what to do with a fridge.

My fridge is haunted by another fridge.
The fridge of my fridge's nightmares who won't let it sleep at night.

My fridge is haunted by me who is haunted by it.

My fridge is haunted by the sign that says **do not enter**.
Do not disturb, the maid should come back later.

MY Body

MY body has turned against me. MY body has decided that it wants to be on its own, it wants to become something else, something outside of me, it is breaking away.

I stubbed my toe, but instead of a bruise it broke. Sideways, straight out. I was too nervous to notice and ignored it until people kept asking about my toe and my limp. It's in these days, I would tell them, but it wasn't in, I was the only one in pain.

MY body has told me that it has better things to do than lug around my pain. It doesn't feel responsible for holding me together anymore, that not much of me was together anymore. MY body has informed me that I am to start shedding my skin.

I fell on the floor, but instead of just skinning my knee, a whole part tore off. Clean from my red insides, I leaked and leaked and people asked if I was okay and I said yes, worse has happened. They remember my broken toe. I remembered my broken toe. All my ghosts are leaking out, I reassured them, but I don't think they cared.

MY body is red and bloody, even the outside. MY body wants to bleed, it wants to bubble, it wants to deflate. MY body wants banana bread and new shoes. MY body wants to go to sleep, but my insides won't be quiet.

I start to laugh, but I cannot stop. The joke wasn't that funny, people said, but I just keep laughing. I am wheezing; I am breaking down from the inside out. My laugh is high pitched; it is a siren that wards people off. It won't turn off, and people are running. They are turned off.

MY body is self-sabotaging. MY body is trying to flip off the light switch, but I am the light switch, and I want to stay on. MY body has become a decaying coffin that is trying to bury me deep inside. MY body is becoming maggots and worms. I want to crawl out, but it is too late to jump ship.

I want someone to fuck, to fuck out this crisis, to fuck the ghosts so hard that they run from my mouth and never come back. I make plans to fuck a friend, but as soon as they enter me, I eat them. It starts at my vagina, it grows teeth like in that shitty movie, but then my mouth joins in and rips them in half. Double penetration, eating both ends, I cannot stop they taste so good.

MY body wants to be left alone. MY body wants to live under a rock, on top of a rock, inside of a rock, anywhere in solitude. MY body is aching, it is tired, it is ready to go to sleep, but I say wake up, I know you can hear me. MY body is angry, it is molting, it is molten lava. MY body is sad; it wants to hide so no one will see it cry.

I try to open a door, but MY body slams the door onto me. Most people would cry, would bruise, but MY body has other plans. I burst into laughter when I realize half my finger is missing. I pick it up off the floor and eat it. If it won't stay on me, then it will stay inside me. The fingernails are always crunchy.

MY body wants to go home; it doesn't want to stay out late. MY body doesn't want to be a cannibal, but it loves the taste of flesh. MY body is gross and full: it is bloated and all consuming. MY body is stuffed. MY body is stuffing.

I try to tie my shoes, but I cut off circulation. I don't untie them, I just watch as they fill with blood, as the circulation cuts off, as my toes go numb, as they swell and as they turn black, as they fall apart, clean break. No more broken toes.

MY body wants to be sent back to the factory. MY body is dysfunctional; it has been tricked into thinking it was supposed to work, but it cannot. MY body no longer has a warranty: it dried up when my mom died, it dried up when the ghosts moved in, it dried up when I let people touch me, it dried up when I started smiling.

I tried to eat my applesauce in peace, but my brother took it. I tried to get it back, but I fell off my ladder, into the wall, and cracked my head open. I tried to sew it back together, but I am no doctor, I couldn't do it, and my brain is leaking out into me.

MY body is happy. MY body can finally be at peace, with as much working brain as it has left, with no more fingers or feet, with a broken body, with pieces of me missing never to come back. MY body is a hermit crab, and it has found its new home: broken and shattered and red, it has decorated well.

On or Off

I wanted to turn the lights off, but then it would be dark. If I let it
be dark, then I can't see. If I let it be light, then they'll see me. Maybe,
though, then I could see them. But the dark, the dark, the dark would
be too much. In the dark the noises don't have a cause, no location, they
just echo and expand and absorb me.

The light, the light, the light will let me see the noises. The dust
floating and stirring. Forming eyes and eyes and eyes. The cat's eyes
outside and the eyes inside my mind. The light that could illuminate
too much, could show too much, could become everything. I can hear
the plants outside mocking me. Laughing at me. On, off, on, off, they
laugh. I don't know why I planted them. The company, I guess, but I
was a different person then. Then I was me. But now they only laugh
and mock. I can hear them, so I'm boiling water. The loud screeches

calm me, silence the plants, and annoy the neighbors. They won't call the cops anymore, though. I only scare the cops but not enough to make them help me. So the teakettle will boil and burn, and tomorrow or next week or next month I'll get a new one. It depends when I want tea. There it is. The noise. I turn the lights on, but the eyes start to stare. They look at me, in me, toward me, but through me. I turn them off and grab the doorknob. I'll leave, I'll run away. Past the cat, past those snickering plants, but I can't. Oh, that neighbor is watching again. Fetishizing my worry, whacking it to the strobe lights of my kitchen—I know it. I can see his mouth on the floor and his eyes out of his head. I can't. Not today. Maybe tomorrow or next week or next month when I want tea.

I miss the taste of tea. The soggy leaves floating in my cup, saying hello, waving to me, smiling. I miss the warm water and small cups. The only tea I drink now is from the tub. When I can't leave and need the leaves, I fill it, in the dark—hidden from those eyes so they don't steal my secrets or pee in my tea. I fill the tub and dump in the leaves. Crispy, chewy, delicious. The big batches and my empty mouth. Oh, how I miss the little cups. The little cups pouring over my naked body soaking up the tea, hiding.

One day I'll want it bad enough. One day I'll turn the lights on, or off. I'm not sure yet, but one day I'll make up my mind and I'll kill the cat and eat those judgy plants, rip out the neighbor's tongue, and buy a new teakettle. One day, but I'm not sure yet. Maybe tomorrow or next week or next month. Whenever those eyes leave. Or maybe when I want tea bad enough.

Flyswatter

Sometimes my ghosts like to hide inside flies. I never know until I swat them, and the ghost falls out bruised and sad. I told them to stop hiding inside the flies or they'll die, but they tell me it's more fun than death.

Sometimes I can catch them doing it. I see a swirl of white that seems to plunge and vanish itself inside a fly the size of a horse. Fruit flies are for sad baby ghosts. I've decided to invest in an electric flyswatter to make it hurt more; ghosts are afraid of electricity. Ghosts are afraid of pain.

I don't know why they insist on hiding. It feels like some sort of hide and seek, but nobody really wins. Sometimes kids' games are only made to annoy parents, but at least kids don't usually die during them.

I don't think that the fly-ghost and the ghost-ghost become one ghost because I am not convinced that flies are meaningful enough to conjure up ghosts and make them fall out. The life span of a fly is less than a month and that would be too many fly-ghosts to count. Perhaps there is an equation for when a fly-ghost will exist, but first, there needs to be a fly that is worthy enough.

Sometimes I like to pop the flies like balloons and watch them deflate and flop around as they shit out the ghosts of my friends and family and butlers and cats. Sometimes I try to catch them in my mouth and chew on them really hard until they cry uncle and I spit them out and laugh at them. I don't think they like this.

Sometimes I think this whole fly thing is their way of telling me they'd rather be alive than living with me, but ghosts don't get to be alive. It's death or flyswatters. Sometimes I think that when I'm a ghost, they won't be my friend anymore. I'm still holding out hope of becoming a vampire.

I might start keeping the flies inside jars and letting them rot inside there until they die and erode and the ghosts become claustrophobic in their tiny jars. I would keep ten of them inside one small jar and watch them try to fight their way out of it: just like the flies, just like the humans, just like when they were alive. My only fear is when the jar falls off the shelf, when they end up inside me, when I become the jar in which they are fighting.

Stitches and Shells

Sometimes I like to play doctor and give myself stitches. I always think they're dissolvable until I realize they were never medical grade; I am only in training, and they do not dissolve.

Sometimes I like to lick the needles to sanitize them with my saliva before I slide them through my thin skin, my voluminous skin, my sticky, sticky skin. Always always always turning red.

Sometimes I like to ask for volunteers, but nobody comes. Sometimes my friends will seep out of my skin, and I have to lock them back inside. If anyone sees them, then they'll know I am too popular; they will not want to join them. I always seem to have a case of deceit.

I like the smell of rubbing alcohol, but I'm not an alcoholic. Sometimes I like to give myself papercuts and bathe in it so I can be the burn and the calm and also the adrenaline. Sometimes it makes me cum.

Sometimes I like to paint my body and run around outside at night, usually around 2:14 a.m. because most people are asleep. Anyone who is awake then is free to join. I wish I could cover myself with Vaseline and pretend to be a slug and sneak into people's houses and become their pet. Most people find slugs to be disgusting, which is nothing new for me.

Sometimes I wish I could crawl into a turtle's shell to find a new home, but then I would have to crawl out of my skin and detach my spine, which is such a burden. I'm sure my friends that I keep stitched inside me wish I would do this so they could join me and we could all live in turtle shells instead of my shell, but none of them have spines, so it is much easier for them.

Sometimes I wish I could stitch together my hands to make one long snake arm, but this would require additional hands that I do not have.

The Winds

The winds out at sea don't point in the right direction. They do not take me anywhere. They do not know where they are going. One is going left but not pushing me that way. They never had a conversation, but I am stuck inside of them.

I can't sleep without a night-light on. Not on this ship with the winds that don't speak. Sometimes I can feel the winds slither up my bed, crawl next to me, and snuggle. I know it's the winds because it all happens so fast and then never exists.

I used to have a crew on my ship. I used to employ people who made money, who had families who they loved. I used to have responsibilities to those families that I never knew, but the winds took them all, and now they've all become the winds.

I don't know why they didn't want me. I'm not quite sure what I did wrong. All I ever wanted was to be out at sea, past the edge of my sheets, and inside the water, but the winds say no, stay, don't go anywhere. They force me into this bed, into this curse, into the rocking of the ocean that I'll never find. They won't let me go anywhere. That's why they won't talk.

If they talked, then I would talk; then they would get to know me; then we could be friends, and they'd feel too bad to leave me stranded out at sea, inside my blankets, muffled under winds and water. If they talked, then we could all get tea, we could have slumber parties, I could get to know the families of the winds that I once employed. If they talked, they could love me, I could love them, we could be a family of our own, but families always die.

I am not trained to sail, I am not authorized on the sea, this isn't my ship, I am no pirate. One day I came out and I've been too scared to leave my sheets and pillows. Sometimes when the sky gets angry, I put on puppet shows, and these puppets talk to me like it's not just me talking to me. These are the saddest days.

Alone at sea I am starving. Alone at sea I have to kill fish and rats and bugs to stay alive. Alone at sea I drink my own pee; I filter it in my shoe. Alone at sea the sun shines so bright that it tries to melt off my skin; I close the shades. Alone at sea I spin in circles until I puke and the winds laugh.

I think one day my steering wheel went missing, the masts deflated, and my bed went to the cleaners. I must have left it outside to dry when the rain began. The rain has never stopped. It turned my bed into a sailboat, my legs into anchors, but I cannot steer them without my wheel. I am scared I will drown. I am scared I will like it. I know the winds will do it.

I think I heard once that if you die at sea, you are destined to become a wind, but they do not want me to; I think I may have made that up to make myself feel better.

I cannot think of where I could have put it, that darn steering wheel. I'm not sure when it washed away. I didn't think you could dismantle a boat that doesn't exist.

Maybe the raccoons took it before the storm, hoping to find a home. Most likely it was just water and mold and winds that took it over. Less likely is that I put it outside to begin with. Maybe it's just floating inside my house, hiding from my bed that is slowly becoming the sea.

I think that if I remember hard enough, slow enough, closely enough that one may appear. If I concentrate, if I beg, if I sacrifice a fish or a rat or bug, my steering wheel may miss me enough to come home.

Would that be fair? Leaving its new home to come to mine? Who would it leave? The fish that steered it to school? The child who needed a raft? The family who just needed direction? The winds that need to learn right from left? But without it my boat will sink; I am only a fish, a child, a one-person home, a queen-sized bed, a few family. Who needs it more? I'm sure if it were me that it would have come home by now.

That is a lie. I'm sure the winds have taken it, will take it, won't let me see it. If I need it, then my bed will sink, if I don't get it, my sheets will get wet, the winds and the ghosts and the ghouls of the sea can eat me. I'm sure they have stolen it.

Nest

She wore gloves on her hands, but not to protect them from the germs and grime from the money to books to illness to mouth to cough, cough to book to rack. She wore gloves on her hands because he wouldn't touch her if she had been somewhere else. She was a robin's egg, and he stood watching, testing her love as if he hadn't touched a skank's ass the other night. Hypocrisy is the foundation of trust. She crossed the names off the list—done, done. And he waited in his nest for her to return.

She laid awake in her nest, perched above the ants and bugs that she feasted on. She looked at them living lives with fingers. Lives that had fingertips and fingerprints and fingers that separated and grew and stretched far beyond their measly nests. These fingers were narrow and fat and short and endless. These fingers grew out of their eyes and ears and had no limits. Some of these things she watched were all fingers, whereas she was just a lady wearing gloves. This lover of hers, this man with a nest full of skanks, wore boots. His boots were long and heavy and hard to knock off his feet, but they were not a part of him. These skanks he brought home could slip them off with ease, but her gloves were stapled to her skin, oozing blood and hard to look at. At night while he slept, she imagined what fingers were like. If she also had fingers, she could pull off the boots of her lover and use them to kick them out of her nest so they could fall to their deaths. But she couldn't. The staples, of course. The goddamn staples that jutted out of her, telling people not to touch, not to step any closer. No, these staples were poison to herself and those around her. Crusted, oozing, dripping, wet, and salty.

But she still worked. She had to work to pay for the nest the skanks and her lover lived in. She organized books by name and numbers and a system she had to get a degree in just so people could take these books, fuck them up, and return them. The staples in her gloves, in her skin, in her bones, cut the pages sometimes. Cut them to pieces so she would just shove those books under her dress and hide them until the end of the day. When the day ended and people and things left and all that was left was her, the books and the shreds of books past she would chew them up in preparation to add them to her nest.

This nest, the nest, her nest was all she really cared about. Her nest, this nest, the nest that she had spent years with, chewing up these ripped books and adding them in, filling in holes, creating bedrooms, bathrooms, parlors, and game rooms. Even a room for her man with the boots to stomp around in with his skanks. She didn't mind that too much. She would rather work on the nest, her nest, this nest than try to rip off his boots and massage his feet. But that doesn't mean she didn't ever want to.

That is where the problems arose. When one day inside the nest, this nest, her nest he did not stay in his room—he paraded around shoeless and without fear—she, instead of building him into the room, into a homemade casket, decided to stuff him under her skirt and hide him away from those skanks. She wasn't sure if he could breathe under there; she wasn't sure if she wanted him to. So she clenched really tight until he got sucked up higher. Higher. Until she could taste his ugly feet. Then she could feel his disdain mix with relief. She thought those skanks would finally leave.

Those skanks could smell him, though. Those dirty, tired, old feet permeated the air, and they sniffed him out like hounds. Under her skirt, up her legs, and into his hiding space they went. Invasive, intrusive, and just inconsiderate. That's when she grew fingers. She could feel bones sprouting and skin ripping. So off came the gloves. This little lady we so admire tore the staples out, oozing and gushing and bloody, and ripped off her gloves until she was bare, until all those little people were inside out and inside of her dirty little glove, stapled together and hidden in her hiding space. There, she could finally keep an eye on them.

The Truth in the Window

I feel like static. Not like fuzzy boundaries and miscalculated targets, but like separate pixels that never want to touch. Never will touch.

I smell cantaloupe and daydreams and feel foggy, heavy, wet. My eyes glued together through fear and reluctance. I can hear my cat meowing.

My favorite thing about cats is that they'll eat you if you die. They're honest and up front. They just want to live at all costs.

I'm fed up that my cat is an alien and won't tell me. She assures me that she'll eat me when I die in my apartment alone, but when it comes to her staring at me all night, conversing with her alien family and dreaming of probing me, she decides not to be honest.

It's unfair that I have to feed an alien whom I'm sure could do it herself if she weren't in a disguise. I think she's hiding it from me because I can't keep a secret, but I would try much harder to keep her secret than someone else's. I like her more.

Her breath smells like frogs and eggs, and I can hear her tone change at the same time I feel eyes on me. If I turn around then I can confirm it, but then I might see aliens. I might see her become an alien. I might learn too much, and then they'll have to kill me, and my mom already killed herself, so I don't know if my sister could take it. But if I stay here hiding my breath, then soon they'll find out I'm only pretending to be asleep. Or maybe I'll fall asleep.

I wonder if she's always been an alien or if she was replaced at some point, and while she was in the shelter she was told to choose me. Maybe I'm overreacting, but I can hear the noises outside my window, and it's not rain or cars or feet or people or my cat eating. It is the inexplicable and undeniable noise of aliens.

My cat is always on edge, and I've come to believe it's because she's an alien. She's always about to be found out, and that's why she's cross-eyed. She's just as paranoid as me because we both know the trust we have is flimsy and built off treats and pretending to listen.

I feed her tuna fish for dinner sometimes even though I know she doesn't like it. I do the same with turkey. Soon she'll go on a hunger strike, and that will signal her family, and then I'll be abducted because I wouldn't buy her only chicken.

There is a slight chance I'm delusional and my cat is only a cat, but it's so rare that cats are really cats nowadays. Even slimmer that I chose a cat who is just a cat. Slimmer even yet that a cat who is just a cat chose me. There's also a chance I don't own a cat and I'm just dreaming or hallucinating because no one would tell me if I never came down from the bad shroom trip when I peed my bed about seven times. Maybe my alien cat would tell me.

I think that the time is coming when I just have to do it. Face my death or my delusion. When I was younger I used to talk to an alien at my house in North Carolina. I would run to my parents' bed, lie down, and look across into my own room where a young alien child was staring at me. No words, only telepathy, but it always disappeared when I got too close. I'm thinking now that it was my cat when she was younger. Telling me that one day we would be together. One day she wouldn't have to hide. My cat is pretty old, so it checks out.

If I could really trust her then I'd ask her, but I already know she would only say meow. I guess I'll have to look.

My Arms

My arms are growing. They're oblong snakes biting my wrists. My arms are dragging behind me. My arms are dragging me behind. My arms behind me. I'm having a hard time understanding these things. I'm having a hard time understanding how they became what they are. They're longer than my legs and are tangling below me. I try to move them, to untangle, to de-knot, to deconstruct this construction of mess and snakes, of poison and venom.

I trip over these arms. They get in people's way and they don't like it. I'm trying to tell them sorry, to shake their hands and apologize, but my arms are too heavy to move. I'm out of breath trying to lug around these things, these monsters, these creatures that I think are mine. I'm wheezing and sad and happy. People avoid me, I avoid people. These arms create a line—do not cross, or the freak may attack. Downside: no one wants to hold my hand anymore.

When my arms sprouted they scared my friends. They scared my lover, who scared me off. These snakes are too heavy to slap them across the face. My hands too pointed, too trapped to stay steady enough to show my anger. These arms are a curse that I can't control.

They say don't bite the hand that feeds, but my hands can't lift themselves up to feed me; they're too far away to bite. I have to eat my food out of a bucket like a pig. No knives, no forks, no spoons. Teeth, teeth, mouth, tongue, eating and chewing. Consuming. My arms sitting next to me absorbing the food.

My arms are too long to clean at night. They're infected and crusty. They ooze out liquids I didn't know were inside of me. The white teeth of the snakes leaking out, drooling, falling apart and shedding their skins. Me watching, wishing I could douse them under hot water, but my hands are too heavy to turn the faucet on.

I'd kill myself if the arms could move. I would wrap them around my neck, a boa constrictor squeezing out the guts of the rat until it shits itself out. But my arms are too long, too heavy, too meaty to kill me.

There was a point, I believe, when they were just the right length, when they could move and wiggle and reach. That point is long gone because now I need a bed just for them. They hit the bottom of mine and keep going. I woke up with spider bites and dust coating my fingertips. So I got my arms a bed that sits below mine. A doggy bed for my snake arms.

My arms are becoming me. I fear that soon I won't be able to stand, that soon I will have to roll around on the floor, down the stairs, across the hall, through the streets until I can find a doctor willing to take them off. What would be better? No arms or long arms? Either way they're useless. If you cut them off then I will be a snake, still. Wiggling my way through this unforgiving snake world. Full of snakes, hating snakes, being snaked, killing snakes.

I guess I will wait until they fall off themselves. It will have to happen. They'll become so long, so heavy that my bones will crunch and tear, the flesh ripping, shredding itself away from myself. The snakes disconnecting, running away. No legs, but body squirming and wiggling and running. My flesh molting. The pain will be normal. The pain: a small price for freedom.

Maybe I could gnaw them off. Biting until they leave. Would they fight back? Would these snakes attack me, bite me? Will they win? They couldn't—they're too lazy and fat and heavy to fight back.

Will I thank me? Will I be happy being a snake girl rather than a snake holder? Probably not. There is no winning when you didn't ask for arms in the first place.

How to Rob One's Body

1. Empty It

When I was younger I tried to rob my body. I starved it for a while, and when people caught on I decided to rub the inside of my throat until the inside became the outside. I miss those times when I could decide what went on inside my body. When I could sit for days and feel my skin tighten around my bones. The delicious raw meat starving, slabbed on top of my fragile, exposed bones. I could feel my body talking to me and I could feel my raw chicken skin dying and dying. My body, then, was too weak to run away.

But like any fun we have as kids, parents ruin it. They made me force food into my stomach. Force fat into this body: foie gras. They also made me put away my toys before I was done playing, in bed by eight.

Grounded for coming home late, cell phone taken away for talking back.

Parents ruin fun.

●   ●   ●

To Acknowledge the Fears

Have your feet ever left you? Have they ever kept walking while you turn, open a door, and head to your desk? Today mine tried. I tried to pull them back, reattach, and guide them to my classroom, to my desk, to my agenda. Well, just when I thought I had control, they took off. Suddenly, I felt myself *walking*. And I just kept walking. And this anxiety inside me bubbled and bubbled, and I just walked faster— not quite at the jogging pace of robbing a bank but just below that, walking as if I was jaywalking past a cop car.

I was robbing my body.

You never think about it, do you? Who owns your body? I'm not sure. Truthfully, I guess it's kind of an exchange. You live inside your mama, so she owns you for a while. Then you go right into school. Wake up at six, in bed at eight. So the school, or maybe the government, owns you for a while. But now I'm twenty-one, and my feet don't know which way to go—they don't know who to listen to anymore. I'm not sure they ever saw me as an authority.

2. Remember It

Before I even knew my body wasn't mine I tried to rob my body. When I was younger I used to take my clothes off and run around naked, masturbating in stores and restaurants. So young that the only memories I have of this are implanted through stories. I think even then I wanted to claim myself. Maybe that's why we wet

54

ourselves. Claiming ourselves, smelling like our own urine to ward off others.

· · ·

To Acknowledge the Challenge

I want to stand still, so I do. I'm robbing my body and I want to stand still. I want to stand and *look*. Not just stare blankly but look into this world I just happened upon. I want to look at lovers fighting and people picking their noses in secret. I pick my nose in secret. Truthfully, I think everyone does.

3. Carve It

I also used to cut myself open. Of course, this was in hopes of robbing my body. To bleed until the contaminated blood was gone, down the drain, out of me. I always had such a respect for medieval medicine. I wanted to slice off the parts of me that I did not like. Open my chicken skin, separate the layers, dump out my fattened liver until I turned red. Red. Heal and move on—perform the surgery elsewhere until my body was my home.

Parents ruin everything.

4. Amputation

I used to eat the hands and feet off my Polly Pockets. I liked the taste of the smooth plastic and I liked how they looked amputated. My sister did not like that too much. She preferred her Polly Pockets with hands and feet, but I had robbed their bodies. I guess, in some way, I had robbed my sister's as well. I had altered her path, I had decided for her that no longer would her Polly Pockets walk on their own. I can remember her tears, her eyes, my confusion. Did everyone not want the same things as me? How could someone long for something other than the taste of Polly Pocket? Perhaps, I hadn't saved her a bite.

I ruin some things.

5. Violate It

When I was fourteen I had sex with someone I didn't really want to, but felt I had to. I let them rob my body so that I could keep them. They promised that sex with them was basically waiting until marriage because everyone meets their spouse when they're fourteen. They left. Boys ruin everything.

When I was sixteen my best friend touched me when I said no, and she wouldn't stop until I fell asleep. Her slender fingers I once loved becoming poison darts. Girls ruin everything.

I forgave her. I took fault for thirty percent because I kissed her and changed my mind. I robbed thirty percent of my body, but the rest was stolen.

•   •   •

Tempt It in Acknowledgment

I kept walking, but my legs were so, so tired, and my anxiety was both high and low. It's exhilarating, you know, robbing your body. It's also terrifying. I should have been in class. I should have been doing homework. I probably should have been doing just about anything other than walking or standing or looking.

So I sat.

Because sitting *is* different from walking or standing or looking.

Oh goodness, I forgot how amazing it was to sit. How relieving it is to rest your feet—and they did. They didn't try to run off of me this time. They stayed and we bonded, laughing about the times we tried to team up and the times we fought.

6. Push It—Harder

I used to run cross country. I was good too. I got my first mile down below five minutes. The fresh air, the wind, the trees. My dad called it the rich hippie sport, which is true. I ran until my knees buckled. Very literally too. My knees stopped being knees, and so I had to stop running. My body robbed itself right from under me and left me behind. It's sneaky like that; just when you think it's on your side, it ruins everything. Bodies ruin everything. Maybe it was revenge, maybe it was a call for help, maybe it was just being spiteful.

•   •   •

Acknowledge the Fight

Just as I thought we were starting to get along, we started to fight. You see, I had work and I didn't want to call out so close to my shift. I told my legs we were going this way, and they said no. They got up and walked away and left me behind—sitting on that park bench.

7. Proclaim It

So I yelled.

I screamed for them to come back, to listen to me. I screamed like a deranged, jealous girlfriend, and they just stuck their tongues out at me and kept walking. People stared. Oh boy did they stare at this weird girl yelling at her legs, but that didn't snap me back. No, I wasn't going to let *them* win. I sat and seemed crazy, but I wanted to win and go to work.

So I got up. I stood and began walking back, but I had no legs, so I just started crawling. I crawled almost ten feet, and someone came to help me up. I told them no. I said this was between me and my legs. It was. I didn't need to stand. I would crawl around work all day if it meant that I would win.

People ruin everything.

They overreact.

They looked at me like my sister looked at her Polly Pockets—sad, concerned, and annoyed that they had to deal with it. But I have feet—I have legs—they just don't listen. They work; they just don't listen. You could see them if you looked: they're ahead of me—running, yelling, being obnoxious.

•　　•　　•

Finish It Off

But they don't listen either. Here I am waiting for my mom to come sign me out of this hospital because I'm not "of sound mind," but it's not me: it's my legs. The doctor robbed my body and will only give it back to my mom—an exchange. An arranged bond of body and mind.

So I stand. And I run.

And finally, your body has been robbed.

Soil and Sands (Yum, Spit)

I do not have a garden. All of the ground is pavement and asphalt. It hurts when my feet touch it: the sun has boiled the rocks, and my skin melts, seasoning the scorching sands.

I do have a patio. A blissful square in which I have created a pile of soil, a nest of bugs, and a farm full of manure. I do not mind the smell.

On my patio I want to harvest a feast for my family. I want to dig up the wolf spiders and rollie pollies and put them in a bowl to live together. I want to plant trees and bushes, I want to plant basil and mint, I want to plant flowers that won't ever stop blooming no matter how many times I forget to feed them.

I do not have shade for my patio. I don't own an umbrella. I do not have a watering can.

I spit on the flowers and soil until I have run out, until it is drenched. Sometimes I run out and have to invite my friends over. They love my spit parties; they say they wish I had done them always. If it is not too late to start always, then I think I always will now.

I have planted a tree that tells me the weather. Or makes the weather. I ask it what is on the menu today. It tells me sun and sun and heat like all the other days, and nothing will change, stop asking; it is sun sun sun sun no fun in this sun.

I have planted my friend as a scarecrow. They sing loudly and angrily. Their favorite choice is Nordic death metal. The crows are not scared; they are friends, and this is acceptable.

I have planted seeds that I hope to turn into food, which will let me harvest a feast and bring my family back. They have left for a different farm, a different patio with less Nordic death metal. I think I can win them back. If I had food they would come back, I tell myself. I hope it is true. The foods I have planted are cucumbers and beets and rice and wheat and ham and corn and pumpkin and sugar cane and bean bushes. It will taste great.

I do not have a gardener. It is only me. I feed it cow poop and human poop and sometimes chunks of cat poop. I throw my eggs in and burnt quiche and sometimes my first borns. I once put my shoe out, and the patio vomited; my feet smelled terrible. I refuse to feed it chocolate or ice cream—I do not like sweets.

I special order my groceries to feed the garden. They only like organic, non-GMO food because it reminds them of a simpler time when lies smelled so decent. They do not eat them: they absorb and desorb and laugh at them. I join in.

The harvest is coming in the following weeks. I believe it will only take a month this year. I must collect all the specialities, pray to the gods, and perform my five-hour sacrifice ritual in which I kill myself through the use of small needles that I insert in my body until I have a heart attack and die from shock. I then must let sepsis seep in and rebirth myself out of my womb, becoming my own mother. I must then start a fire and rise from it as my farmland grows and expands and the patio thinks it is the world even if my neighbors refuse to give up ownership of theirs—for the purposes of a ritual, it is all within the belief of the believer. This creates trust and durability in my land, bonding between me and the food. A week after I will invite my family for the feast they have always wanted. I am sure they won't come.

Roommate

"There is a pig who lives with me. They do not like the taste of mud. I asked them to move out, but they refused. I cannot complain: they do the dishes. I'm not sure when they moved in. I'm not sure how they saw my ad on craigslist. I do not remember a time without them anymore.

When I go grocery shopping I take their list. They always want seventeen bags of carrots and twelve cases of crackers. Ritz crackers, specifically. I never know what I want, but I buy things that always seem like a good idea and never are.

I like to write on the toilet, but they yell because I take too long. I'm doing my homework. Don't do it in the bathroom. I have to do it in the bathroom. I concentrate better in there. Less breaks, more focus. They always interrupt me.

In the morning we do our makeup together. Theirs always turns out better. I think they used to be related to or family friends with some fancy person. They own twelve different makeup brushes. I use my fingers.

Every Wednesday we have wine together and order pizza. I like pepperoni, but they like olives with pesto. We have to order two because neither of us will compromise. Ever. I always thought pigs were cannibals. They tell me that they're reformed.

I work part-time at a coffee shop and do tutoring. I'm waiting for something to spark my interest and then I'll commit to it. People included. They work full-time at some agency as a secretary. I don't think they like me very much.

I like to gossip about my parents because they suck. They always smell like eggs and they think I have no joy in life. I don't think the pig cares much about me, or for me. I think they mostly only care about skin care and hair care, which causes me a great deal of stress. We are supposed to be teammates. That's what roommates do. But my roommate is a little self-involved.

I think this is where our issues truly come to light. They never listen to me unless it is an insult to them. The only way to communicate with a pig is to tell them they've plateaued. They only know how to speak through insults. They tell me I've only been dipping since college. They think it hurts me, but it cannot because I already knew that.

On Saturdays, I always want to get brunch and bottomless mimosas, but they don't drink mimosas. That means I have to drink enough for the both of us and throw up by five p.m. They think I'm disgusting, but I'm frugal.

This Saturday, though, they brought a friend. They didn't even ask. All they did was videotape me and laugh, and I couldn't help but keep drinking. I always thought I was funny, but I think, in reality, I am only stupid, which always gets people to laugh.

Usually, on Sundays I watch football. So does the pig. This is the only thing we agree on.

This Sunday, though, they brought their friend back and showed her around the apartment. This seemed fishy to me because they never had a friend before me. They then told me they are kicking me out and won't let me re-sign the lease. I tried to tell her that they can't do that because I'm the one that found them on craigslist, but they told me they're the only one paying rent.

I think that in a past life we were friends, and I must have murdered their parents and that is why they hold so much disdain for me. I've tried apologizing, but they say it's never for the right things, but I don't know what could be more important. This is why I've asked them to come to therapy with me today."

The Diagnosis

My knees are infested with termites and rot.

That is what the doctors have told me.

They ache when I sleep and I repair them in the morning.

The doctors tell me that it could be the running or genetics or perhaps pests.

It wasn't the drugs, I tell them.

They look at me like they want to believe.

My knees look crooked and crippled.

That is what the doctors have told me.

You have years to live, they say.

But your house is being eroded due to the foundation.

That is what the contractor tells me.

He is also talking about my knees.

My knees look like socks filled with chewed rice.
They taste like human flesh, a cannibal told me.
My knees work as if they were seventy.
My age is only twenty-two.
Sometimes when I bend down, I stay down.
That is an elevator joke.
Sometimes when they go pop people duck.
That is a gun joke.
I've never owned a gun; most likely I never will.
My knees are wooden; I am a puppet.
This is what Geppetto told me.
My nose is so small it may never grow; my sense of smell is bad.
My knees are out of gear.
This is what my mechanic told me.
Sometimes the house starts leaning, and you have to tear the whole thing down.
My knees are not the worst of it.
This is what my dead mother assures me.
She was sent to death by her back.
If I die from my knees then we won't be the same.
My knees are annoying to work around.
This is what I tell myself.
This is what I hide in my secret bookshelf.
Inside there is a wall of knees.
I am a collector.
My knees are infested; I am buying a new house.

My Friends

I wish I were never friends with people I liked. Instead, I wish I were friends with people I could murder and stuff in my walls. Instead of liking people and making connections, I would rather adorn my insulation with skin and bones. If the skeletons of my mind could become a reality, then inside me wouldn't be so scary.

If I were only friends with people I hated then I would always think they suck. I could complain about their complacency and their hatred of true art. Instead, I am sure they all meet to complain about me.

If I hated everyone then I could become a hermit crab and traverse the sands of beaches until someone plucked me up and kept me as a pet until they stopped feeding me and I starved. Finally at peace.

I wish I were friends with people who had no talent so that I was always better than them. If I could be the best at anything, I would be the best at everything. I wish I were friends with people who were always in awe of me, instead of me being the aw in them.

If I had more talent or more bones then I could be friends with talented people without dissolving, but until then I am a puddle of slime and goo.

I wish I could stand without melting at the sound of words from people I don't know. I wish I didn't respect anyone. I wish I hated my parents.

If I hated my parents then I could become a porn star without disappointing them. If I hated my parents I would be glad my mom is dead and I wouldn't care that my dad is in another state. If I hated my parents I could hate my siblings and smoke cigarettes. I would have stories. People stop caring that your mom is dead after she dies.

I wish that my feet were shaped like oysters so people would be interested in me. If my feet were not feet but just clamshells then I would have a nickname like clam-feet girl, and people would let me be the cool one in a group. If my feet were shucked and sold then I wouldn't have to try so hard to be different; I already would be.

I wish my friends lived in bags so I could be more successful than them. I wish they lugged around potato sacks and hid underneath them when it rained. If they were so poor they had to live out of a sack that was once the home of potatoes, then I could be rich. In comparison.

If I were rich I could be selfless and donate money and everyone would know I'm a good person. I could be the best person by default because my friends only owned potato sacks.

I wish that my friends were all fat because then I would be skinny. If they all weighed one-thousand pounds then I could weigh half that and still be better. If they all weighed one-thousand pounds they may die sooner, too, which leaves me prevailing.

If my friends were fat and I was skinny then I could look at food without hating it. I could be hungry with desire; I could eat without contempt. I could go to the stand and not plead the fifth. I could be alive.

If my friends were all liars then I could tell them the truth—that I hate them—and they'd think it was a joke. If I could hate people without remorse then I could finally collect my skeletons and assemble them into my walls. If I could hate people then they'd have scars and not me. Addicted to blood but too nice to dice.

I wish that my friends would worship me and start a religion in my name. I would write a bible, and the commandments would be easy: be nice, be me, be real. The religion would have millions of followers, and they would say I'm pretty.

I wish my brains were more important than my beauty, but I wish my beauty were more important than my brains. I wish I cared about things in proper proportions. I wish I was a human and not a sack of skin my friends use as potato bags.

I wish my feet were used to walk instead of mope around. I wish my friends could see my feet for what they're worth.

The Lemons, Mmm

There is a woman in my dreams whom I dream of. She is somewhat like a spider and also a cat and also me. Sometimes I see her at the grocery store, mixed among the fruits, always near the lemons. She doesn't seem to want to talk to me. She seems more like a reminder, like a yellow light, like a report card. She doesn't speak, but she stays, always visible.

In my dreams we are sometimes friends, sometimes foes, sometimes almost the same person. In my dreams there are no faces, only holes that lead to bodies that lead to roads of disappointment. In my dreams there are sometimes legs and arms and torsos, but the heads are always elsewhere, always busy; they couldn't make the appointment. In my dreams I stare, longing, wishing I knew what she looked like in reality.

At the grocery store, near the lemons, she seems to be with friends. Always too busy for me but always there to see. She seems to be gloating, to be showing me that she is real enough to exist with the lemons. I think she's trying to make me jealous, if she thinks it bothers me that others know her too, that I didn't just dream her up. Her need to prove her realness drives me insane. I ignore her while she ignores me, but I think we're really side-eyeing each other. I can feel her turn yellow and rotten as she wishes I would pay attention.

This woman doesn't have a backstory, she doesn't have a tragic youth, she isn't someone to care about or feel bad for. I think of her, of who she would be if I could decide her fate. I think of the facts that she wishes no one knew: she clenches her jaw at night, she gets turned on when someone tickles her gently while licking her teeth, she wears a night guard to protect from her teeth wearing away. I don't know about her parents; she doesn't talk. I don't know her favorite color. In the reality where she lives it is all black and white; she never knew what color the lemons really were.

I think she follows me, but it takes her too long to get from place to place, and that is why I only see her at the grocery store and in my dreams. I grocery shop every day because I'm terribly forgetful and not very responsible. I don't even buy lemons, so I don't know why she waits there. The first time I noticed her I had to do a double take, and she whipped her hair over her shoulder like in one of those commercials. She is very conceited.

I think lemons signify the way she views herself in this place of trying to be cheerful, trying to be something that tastes sour but refreshing, something people want when they're hot and need to cool down, the zest that makes fish taste good and the way that people always furnish

71

their apartments with more and more and more lemons. Probably it's just a coincidence.

Sometimes at night in my dreams when I'm dreaming of her, she crawls over my body, and her millions of legs grow new legs and turn into billions and cover me like a blanket. It tickles. I lick my teeth and I open my skin and let her crawl around my insides and tickle my blood. In my dreams we are some new sort of sexual fantasy where we are both fully fulfilled and soaked in my blood and piss and at the end we smoke a cigarette. We share one because we are close and not addicts. In this dream I like to think that in another world, in a different time, we could be lovers, could at least be friends.

She never looks at me the next day. After these dreams she acts like she never entered my dreams, like she never probed my mind and slid through my brain. She acts like she has never seen what it meant to be friends, or foes, or sometimes almost the same person.

In the store we can't look at each other. In the store we are strangers. In the store she begins to look more and more like me. Like a full-grown woman hiding inside the lemon basket.

There Can't Be a Haunting without Orbs
I Have Pictures

There are orbs in my mind, in my souls, in my feet. I see the orbs in all the colors. The yellows and blues and grays. There are orbs in my bathroom, in my kitchen, in my tiny, small hallways that make me claustrophobic. The orbs are eating all my cat food, but I do not think that they are cats. There are orbs in my bed at night, and they don't make enough room for me. The orbs don't like when I sing in the shower, but I do it anyway because I want to. The orbs are mean. They yell at me; they don't let me sleep. They think they know better; they do. They know all my secrets. They know about my night-light and my horrible BO. They know that I call my therapist every morning to remind them to get up. They know I don't have a therapist and I make it up. They know that I want to go home but that I stay out anyway. They think they know who I am, and they probably do. There are orbs in my pajamas, but I told them to ask me before they borrow my clothes. They never ask; they don't want permission. They know that I never pay rent on time. They know that I am broke. They know that I wish I could be a porn star. They know about the time I tried to kill myself in sixth grade. They also know you can't OD on gummy vitamins. The orbs are becoming my house; soon I will live inside them, but they know that I never pay rent, so they'll evict me, I'll have nowhere to go, I don't know who invited them here, it wasn't me, it wasn't me, it wasn't me, it wasn't me, it wasn't me, it wasn't me. They know it wasn't me.

Homemade Soup

I don't trust anyone. I don't trust anyone. Not even my cat. She has become such a cunt. It's the smell. The smell of her, of me, of everyone, of all the soups. I don't think I can trust her not to tell my secrets anymore; she is always yapping to those ghosts.

My gardener quit. I think he was sleeping with my mom, and then she died, so he left. He didn't say sorry; he just never came back.

My florist won't return my calls. I don't need flowers; I need a friend, but she tells me that isn't her job. What would I do with flowers since my gardener quit? Nothing. I tell her this, but she doesn't care.

My cat has stopped meowing. She stopped moving. Sometimes her tail will toddle, and that is how I know she wants her evening soup. She doesn't eat it; she swims in it. That is how I know I cannot trust her anymore.

Inside the soup are seventeen carrots, one can of peas, four cans of corn niblets and two cups of water. Bring it to a boil, add a dash of salt, one-third cup crushed red pepper seasoning, and serve. She does not like the taste—too spicy—but she likes to swim around in the pan and take a nap. It's the only exercise she gets so I don't mind.

My pool boy has not quit, but I do believe he is dead. He just stands by the pool, staring at it. I think someone has shish-ka-bobbed him, and he is too afraid to tell me. He's leaving me, too. They all do.

My boyfriend has run off with my sister. And my father. My brother as well. They took my boyfriend's parents and left me. Me and the cat who has become a cunt. I do not know what I did; I deserved an invitation. All I get are postcards saying they are having more fun without me, and they're glad I'm not there. I think this is what all postcards want to say, but usually they're too afraid.

I don't trust them. Any of them. This dumb death and those stupid quitters. All I think is that they must also hate my cat, and that is why they cannot tell me the truth. I think I may learn to trust my cat again; maybe if I start to like her then they will too, and we can be friends again. She has been coming around. The way she talks to the ghosts is much more truthful now. She tells them that she has taken up smoking and that I have become such a cunt, which I have. I knew I always would. They tell her that she should confront me. She is too scared.

Sometimes I will make myself soup but not the same kind I make for my cat. Mine is made of miso broth, one log of tofu (undiced), and seven pounds of scallions. American miso.

I have decided to confront my cat. I tell her I know she has been talking to the ghosts about me. No response. I tell her I know she has been smoking. Meow. I tell her I know she understands me. Nothing. I tell her no more soup until we settle this. She rolls her eyes. I say please. This is when I start crying. She tells me to stop being such a baby. She informs me that this is why everyone leaves. This is why my boyfriend ran off with my sister and father and brother and took his parents. This is why my gardener fucked my mother instead of me. This is why the pool boy won't look at me—shish-ka-bobbed or not. I wipe my tears and thank her. She tells me this is pathetic; she's only known me for a week. It is true: I am pathetic, but it doesn't stop me. Rarely do pathetic people stop.

I've decided to clean my life up. I ask my cat to sleep in my bed at night. She tells me no. She does not like to sleep with strangers. I ask her if the ghosts want to be my friends. She tells me no: they do not like me. I begin to cry, and she walks away.

I've decided to try a new recipe to thank my cat for her honesty. I tell her this is the "you're not a cunt anymore" soup. She meows even though I know we can discuss such things in my language. In this soup I have added one whole canned chicken, cranberry juice cocktail, and two cases of olives. She tells me she does not like olives, and I must take them all out. I do. She never touches it.

I've decided to buy a car, so I call the first car commercial I see and say that I want to buy a car. They tell me no. They have run out of cars for losers who can't even drive to the dealership.

I tell my cat, but she has no pity. I cry and she walks away. I ask her why she doesn't love me, and she informs me that she might love me if I could make a soup worth eating. I'm afraid she has become my abusive husband, but I do not tell her this.

I've decided to buy a diamond collar for my cat. I call QVC and ask for one diamond collar for my cat, and they tell me that is stupid: they do not and would never sell such things. They hang up. Two weeks later I see diamond collars on QVC, so I call to order one. They tell me those aren't meant for human use. I assure them I have a cat; they tell me they don't believe me and hang up.

I'm trying a new soup recipe today. I am going to use twelve fingerling potatoes, eight cloves of garlic, and two whole live octopi. My cat informs me that she does not like octopus. Or garlic. Or potatoes. Or me.

I've decided that my cat has become a cunt again because I can hear her laughing with those ghosts. She stares at the bathtub where they all slit their wrists together, laughing about how much blood there was and how long it took them and how they all wish they could marry a Jonas brother. There are three of them, which means they will not leave one for me. I will be stuck alone. Now I know how Frankie must feel.

I've decided to confront my cat again. I tell her that she didn't save me a Jonas brother. She meows. I tell her I know she can hear me. She says meow. I tell her that isn't a meow. She says meow. I say meow. She says meow. I say meow. She says meow. I say stop it. She says meow.

I've decided to slit my wrists so that the ghosts become my friends. I've made a soup called "time to kill myself" soup. It contains three of my own teeth, chicken broth, a log of raw hamburger meat, and eleven acorns. I get into my bath of broth and slit my wrists. I wake up ten hours later, and my cat informs me that all I did was knick my wrists, pass out, and snore. My cat and the ghosts laugh at me. This is why I don't get a Jonas brother. They inform me that is correct.

I think I must kill my cat. I will poison her soup. Inside this soup I put arsenic, Flavor Aid, and nine bouillon cubes. My cat said she won't eat it because I have poisoned it. She is incredibly smart.

I've decided my cat was never the cunt, but I must have been. I apologize to her; I tell her I know I was wrong and I understand that it was all my fault. I do not blame her or the ghosts. She informs me that she will never forgive me, and I must move out. I am packing my things.

The Addict

I have seeds the size of peanuts that I stick in my ears. When they open, they crawl around until they find a corner that is comfortable. Inside my ears are at least twelve seeds the size of peanuts, and they hatch corn and mold. I am never sure which one it will be, but I am always pleased. This corn, this mold will become my hair. The hair will look like tiny heads on chains that are dangling out of my tiny head on the chain of my body. I cannot cut my hair: I can only retract it by sucking in really hard.

I am not Medusa; no one will turn to stone if they see me. The worst that will happen is you'll be disgusted, which happens all the time. I am not pretty, I barely have a face anymore, my body is mostly avoidance. I am not handy; I cannot change a flat, and no one will hire me because of my looks and smell. I hate showering and so do my tiny heads. I am not terribly nice, I do not like small children, animals bark at me even if they're usually mute, and electronics malfunction out of rebellion.

I once had a date in which they assured me looks didn't matter, and they threw up on sight. Love doesn't happen instantly, but usually vomit is a bad sign. We didn't stop after the vomit; they apologized, and I said it was okay and I was used to it. I am. We had ice cream for dessert, and I didn't see them vomit that time. When I brought them home they told me my home smelled weird, and I told them it wasn't my home. I don't know why I did this. They called the police.

I once had a date in which they left. I have had multiple of these dates.

I once had a date that ended in sex, and afterward they killed themselves, and I didn't blame them. I thought of joining them, but my tiny heads told me they weren't ready to die yet, and I realized that I am more than just me.

I wish upon stars when they pass that I had snakes in my hair because at least that would be useful; I could care for them more easily. I wish that someone would cut them off without killing me, but I know more seeds the size of peanuts would find their way into me. I am addicted to this rebellion of beauty and yet I ache for a way to resemble what you want, what anyone could want, what I want. At least if I were made of snakes instead of tiny heads, I would sound like music instead of mistakes. Then people would listen to me.

If I could make my perfect body, it would change in everyone's eyes. When people described me to each other they would all be confused. I don't know what a perfect mutant looks like, but everyone else has their opinions, and I want to be all of them. I want to be tall and short and thin and thick. I want to have eyes that glisten and eyes that smolder. I want to have teeth that say hello, and I don't want mold and corn growing out of my head in the form of tiny heads on chains. Still, though, I'm the one with the seeds the size of peanuts, I am the one shoving them inside of my ears, I am the one who refuses to suck these heads in.

It is not a curse; it is just genetics. The seeds the size of peanuts cannot be controlled; don't bother asking. If they do not go in, I will shrivel up and die, and the only thing worse than ugly is death, although they feel the same at times. There was no witch who hated my family. I was born out of a puddle, alone and cold. I am just a girl without snakes.

I am just a girl with tiny heads on chains.

I am just a girl.

Charles

There was a small house that sat at the top of a hill. When it rained too much the house seemed to slump back into the dirt, trying not to get wet. The house on this hill tried to act like its shield. It would eat the rain, absorb the wetness, the ground, the stilts that the house sat on, digging into the ground slowly, sliding into the ground—becoming the ground.

This small house on the top of the hill was amongst many on top of many hills. The town that it sat in was very hilly. Not a mountain, not very tall, but bumpy like legs after camping. The hilly town was named Hillside after the hills and also the founder. Very few people lived in Hillside. People found it tedious and bad for their cars. No one lived in the small house that sank into the ground, mostly due to insurance issues, but many people admired it. The durability and loyalty the house had to its hill was unlike others. The residents of Hillside hoped their houses had the same loyalty. They would get down on their knees at night and pray they would never slide off their hill.

A small group of children who were not rebellious but mostly curious would sometimes go to this small house that no one lived in that sat at the top of a hill in a town named Hillside. They would climb the long, blue staircase and find themselves on the porch. While on the porch they could feel themselves sinking into the ground—the weight of something other than the house withering away at its knees. The house was still happy to have visitors. The children would look out on their town of Hillside and find their own houses on tops of hills. They would see their local grocery store, Hanter's. They watched the postal workers drive up and down and up and down and leave presents for all the residents. Sometimes they would catch the mayor sitting in his car getting head from someone they didn't recognize. These children kept notes of what they saw and shared it with their school via Google Docs. They made sure not to share the document with their teachers. This was a children's secret.

The house on top of the hill that was slowly sliding into the earth was happy to hold them. The blue and white paint was chipping away at the edges of the house, and the shutters barely clung to the house, but it did not think about the decay much. Neither did the children. Sometimes in their notes the children would describe the house as if it were their friend. They had named the house Charles. It was the only Charles they knew.

Soon after the shared Google Doc reached a page count of one-hundred, other students went to visit Charles. This made the house more useful. People who used to watch with envy of the house perched on top of that hill now felt like they had a right to see the view from this house on this hill named Charles in the town named Hillside. It seemed as though everyone had visited Charles at least seven times now. The Google Doc had more and more participants, more and more notes. Soon teachers and postal workers and mothers and dogs were able to view and add to the story of the notes from the view at Charles.

Eventually, even the mayor was added to the shared Google Doc, and this is when Charles was demolished. The students tried to protest. They made picket signs and brought chains to tie themselves to the house, but sadly all their parents came at seven and unbuckled them so they could be in bed by eight. Charles was torn down, fumbled and fell down the hill to the bottom of the street, the bottom of the view, the bottom of Hillside. Everyone cried, including the mayor because he understood the beauty of Charles. Still, though, the stilts stood. *No one could demolish those*, the notes read.

My Gaps, the Canyons, and Tar

There is a gap between my teeth that resembles the gap between my toes and the gap between my legs. So much gets lost in there. In all of the theres. The remote to the living room TV has fallen in and won't resurface. It seemed to follow the wrappers from the candy bars I pretend not to have and the children's teeth I attempt to collect—both of which are in hopes of appearing special and sweet. I think it must be stuck with the dust bunnies and video games, decorative pillows, the small bits of glass and wine cork, and of course the batteries. I'm scared, to say the least, that one day this vortex, the trapdoor will open up and try to swallow me as well. Drowning in there slowly but surely, the last thing I'll hear is the TV chattering behind me, always stuck on ESPN because I can't fish this remote out.

The gap between my teeth looks like a canyon, which reminds me of my toes that have valleys between them, hiding horses and snakes and wild cowboys, that brings me to the barren lands of my legs that only contain tar and feathers. From a distance you couldn't tell the difference; you wouldn't want to. You could get lost looking at them, never seeing the tar until you are too close; you couldn't hear the cowboys until it is their last yeehaw, and the canyons look like plains until you've fallen off.

I'm not sure where I left the remote. I could have sworn I was still using it when it had vanished. I can't remember if I was using it as floss or a dildo, but I'm sure it's not in my toes. It would make no sense. Cowboys aren't used to this technology, the snakes couldn't eat it, and the horses would trample it. So I know that it can't be in my toes: the valleys are barren besides the things that live there. My remote is not one of those things.

That leaves my legs and my teeth. Both so versatile, both so relevant, both so possible. I remember so clearly two alternate routes of this poor remote. I was eating popcorn and I had a kernel stuck in my molar. Stuck so deeply in my molar that I couldn't get it out and I couldn't wait any longer, so I grabbed my remote and rubbed it to and fro in my teeth, along my gums, pulling, threading, tearing, gnawing, bleeding until I found that kernel. Every time I got to the right tooth the kernel would pop, would run, would flee to another cliff, another mountainside and hide in the canyon. It wasn't until the ghost in my bathroom sang that I got scared and swallowed it. I hate when she does that; she always wants attention at the worst times. So she sang, I sunk, and with it the remote vanished.

It is just as likely, even more likely, still possible, that that memory is completely made up. It could be between my legs because I remember watching TV and getting really wet when the sexy paint commercials came on, so I took the remote and shoved it up my vagina, rubbing, pulling, moaning, throbbing, bleeding, stretching, ripping, every time I got close to climax the buttons pressing, changing the channel, ruining the mood until that commercial came on again, making me scream, making me drip like the paint, but then that stupid ghost in my bathroom started singing, so I clenched so tight that the remote got lost inside of me. It's always that ghost. She sang, I sunk, and with it the remote vanished.

I'm not sure which one is true and which I'm only dreaming of. My mouth and my vagina hurt just as much, but I only own one remote, so one has to be a trick. I would ask that wretched ghost, but she'll just start singing and won't ever answer. She only replies with "The Star-Spangled Banner" nowadays. I'm not sure where she heard it since I always thought she was Canadian, but I guess you're never as close to your bathroom ghost as you think you are. I've thought of asking my kitchen ghost, but she likes to lie too much. I'm sure she'll say it's actually in my toes when I know that is impossible because my toes feel fine, and the cowboys don't have any questions. I knew I shouldn't have trusted her when she told me my bathroom ghost was Canadian. No one dies and wants to go to the United States.

The tar in the gap of my legs is thick and full of puss. So much gets lost in there, like my cousin and his father, my first boyfriend, spoons, and forks but never knives. There are flashlights of those who couldn't find their way out, there are bones and rattles, porcupines and parsnips. Too many broken bottles and beer cans, but most importantly there might be my remote.

The canyons of my teeth are another story because you can never get anything back from there. At the bottom of these cliffs are blood and beasts, floors full of flesh, floods of human remains. The cliffs collect people and coins, dropped jewels, miscounted napkins at a dinner table. But there, there might be my remote.

There are too many possibilities, and the TV has become so boring, so aged. I see it oozing out oldness with every minute of indecision. Can I even get it back? Could I even enter my gaps without falling in too deep, suffocating, cracking my head, bleeding out? I've never minded losing anything to them before, but there have to be boundaries. Is it worth it to not have to buy a new remote? I've always felt connected to this one; my mother passed it down to me. My mind is heavy with thoughts of the future, thoughts of remotes that don't fall inside my gaps, thoughts and wishes for a ghostless house, but I know both of these will always remain fiction, sadly. Moving feels obsolete.

My eyes are foggy with tired and I know I must sleep and begin my search tomorrow, but the TV is so loud, and I can't turn it down without the remote. The sound is so loud, and the ghost in my bathroom is trying to sing even louder than it; it is unbearable and the ghost in my kitchen is yelling at her. Is yelling at me for losing the remote. Is throwing a temper tantrum. Is being a little brat because she can't think of her lying lies because the ghost in the bathroom is singing so loudly and so poorly. I stand up to yell at her, to yell at both of them. The remote falls out of me onto the floor. Down my legs and to the floor. Then one comes flying out of my mouth. More seem to secrete out of me like sweat. Soon, my house is covered in remotes. The ghosts finally shut up; they are drowning in remotes. Drowning in all the people my gaps have confiscated. My rooms are filling with the things lost in my cracks and crevices. The TV breaks, the remotes are useless, but I fall asleep quickly, violently—at least I will suffocate with all my remotes.

Leaky Leaky Roof

There are legs dangling from my ceiling. They are falling, leaking, seeping from the cracks and crevices. I try to wipe the legs away with my broom, I swat and pull like trying to kill a spider, but they just keep sprouting. Bamboo never stops growing; it just infests and takes over; I think these legs must also be bamboo because no matter how hard I try they won't leave me alone. I think that maybe my neighbors left their sink on. They must have left the sink and bathtub running while they fled town, broke bail, so their human garden grew too much and is taking over. Their legs invading me. When my guests come over I tell them to just ignore the legs, but it is impossible, so they all leave. They treat these legs as if they are mine—unwanted, unneeded, unknown—but these are my neighbors' legs, not mine. I want to shout this at them. I want to go upstairs, kick down the door, and look these legs in the eye, but I'm too scared. The legs have grown six feet long, so their faces must be even bigger. If I go upstairs they may not let me return. I tickle their toes, I lick their feet, but they seem to like it. I've decided to decorate for Christmas, so I give them all pedicures and paint tiny trees on all the big toes. Maybe we can be Friends, and I can negotiate with these terrorists. This dream fades because I can hear them conspiring. They are talking, whispering, yelling, but I do not speak the language of legs. I press my ear against the ceiling, against the soles of the feet, but they just kick me away. I pretend not to care. I pretend not to die of envy. Before I can notice they all run away. I close, I open, and they're gone. I miss their leg hair and their silky knees. My friends have all left. No one is coming. Perhaps, I am sick.

Microslave

There is something living in my microwave. I'm not sure who put it there or when, but I can hear it rumbling around at night. I'm not sure if I'm still allowed to use my microwave anymore because I don't want to harm it. I don't want to become a murderer, a sadist. I'm not sure exactly what it is. I try not to scare it too much, but it always hides. When I hear it roaming around I sneak into my kitchen to try to peek, but the light goes off, and it leaves. Once it hears my toes tapping I can hear it run and hide under the plate, in the wires, behind the lightbulb.

I'm thinking of taking my microwave to a microwave specialist, but I'm not sure that those exist. I think of calling my mother to ask for a recommendation, but I know she is sleeping. I know she has other things to worry about rather than my microwave. I google "microwave specialist" on the internet, and only one thing pops up. It says Ian the

Microwave Specialist, so I call Ian the microwave specialist and make an appointment. He tells me that he only makes house calls and he can arrive in approximately twenty minutes. I tell him that it's midnight, and I don't want to inconvenience him. He asks me why I called him so late then; it must be a microwave emergency. He is right; it is a microwave emergency.

He arrives in twenty minutes down to the millisecond and lets himself in. I point him to the microwave and tell him about the noise it's been making. He asks me to demonstrate, so I imitate the sound that rice makes when spilling on the floor. He tells me that can't be it; he knows that it just sounds like rice spilling on the floor. I try again, but this time I try to resemble how ants must sound when walking on a glass table. He tells me to be quiet; he's heard ants walk across a glass table, and that sounds nothing like it. I tell him that I'm not sure. He assures me that's not what ants sound like. No, I tell him, I'm not sure what sound it makes then. He asks me where I hear it from. My bed, I say. We go to bed. We get in our pajamas and we go to sleep. Soon we hear that noise. That's the noise, I tell Ian. He knows already; he says he's heard microslaves before.

I'm concerned at this point. He knows what he's doing, but all I can do is cry in the corner, so I keep crying, and he tells me to be quiet or I'll scare it off. I tell him I'm sorry I'm a disappointment, and he tells me to be quiet or I'll scare it off. How did you know? I ask Ian the microwave specialist. That's what it always is, he tells me; no one calls me anymore because they all just think it's in their mind, but these little things can be dangerous. Why? I ask him. They start in the microwave, but soon they become everything. He tells me he saw a case where they started to eat the cat, and all they saw was half a decomposed cat next to a pile of microslaves dismantling it. You think that you know why half your food goes missing after you reheat it, but it's always them. He tells

93

me it's a classic mistake. I assure him I won't make this mistake again. He tells me that he knows I won't. I tell him that I know I won't. There is only one way to get rid of them, he tells me. Of course, I say. We eat it, he says. Logically, I say. We prepare a trap of jam, mustard, and water that creates a quicksand the microslave can't escape from. We've got him, Ian says. I smile and try to hold his hand, and for a moment we have done something together. We spend some time cutting the microslave into bite-size portions. Each of the bites must measure out to one square inch each. Conveniently, a microslave stops growing at two inches, so each leg and arm and torso and head only needs to be cut in half. I let Ian do the cutting; I like to watch. We make sure that the blood is presented on every surface in my kitchen, especially the microwave. To ward off others, he says. To ward off others, I agree. We heat a pan with some coconut oil to bring out the sweet flavors of the microslave and sauté him with some salt, pepper, paprika, and crushed red pepper. You're going to make it too spicy, I tell him. No, I won't, he assures me. I watch as the skin crisps like a french fry and the hair sizzles and disintegrates. Soon they look like raisins, like bacon-wrapped dates, like a sweet snack you wish you had more of. We eat them out of the pan, no need to dirty any dishes. He doesn't make them too spicy. It tastes just like it should. I should always have trusted Ian the microwave specialist.

Ian tells me that he must leave. I wonder why. He tells me it's another call. They must be everywhere. They come in clans, they come in cohorts, they come with wagons and horses, and they invade and encroach on everything. No microwave is safe, he tells me. He is so brave. I ask him when he will return. He tells me that I still need to pay him. I give him five-hundred dollars. He tells me he will return when he has taken care of the epidemic. I know this means he will never return.

Smelly Smelly

I should have realized it when he stopped touching me that he was dead. When I was a grape and he was a raisin I should have put it together that he couldn't breathe anymore, the sugar rushed out of him; he shit the bed. That never seemed too far from reality.

I don't know how I didn't realize that his footsteps never made a sound, that he became a whisper at the end of every sentence. I never realized I was the only one hearing him. I wished that maybe everyone else was going crazy, that it wasn't me.

It didn't sink in when his parents stopped calling, when everyone stopped calling, when I got twenty-seven casseroles in the mail. I don't read my mail anymore. I never read it to begin with. The bills were red, eviction notices and bills past due. They told me they were sorry for my loss, but no one cared that I didn't realize he was dead, and my power was shut off.

I should have known the cat hated him because he wasn't real. I should have realized she wanted protection from his hunched back and hollow body. He always felt like a tree in real life, but he became a withered, weathered branch in death.

The smell smelled as if someone had died, but I thought it was just his feet. The food went bad, his sausages crusted and decayed, his Hot Pockets freezer burnt. The mold in my bed grew until I had to sleep on the couch. Everyone was on the couch—my mom moved back in, my cat moved in, my dad came, my siblings came—everyone was crying, and I asked for an extra blanket. Their tears seem to soak through me, not yet reaching him.

The water bill was fifty dollars less. His body soap never ran out, the smell the smell. His deodorant was full, the smell the smell. His food was open, his food was different, no that's my food, why is his food always perfect?

I should have realized I was less happy, but I called it a bump in the road a dry spell one of those days one of those times that people stop having sex I gained weight he is tired also his feet smell so bad I don't feel like it.

I should have known by the time my vagina shriveled up and fell off and rolled around the floor like a marble, but I don't know how to play marbles, so I think my cat ate it.

The time he died is unclear. I think he was killed—by himself or the cat or by me; I may have let him sleep in too late; I think this might be a joke about working too much or a warning about being a musician.

His friends became my friends but then became strangers. When the coroner came and the police came and everyone came, they moved onto the couch with me and my mom and my father and my siblings and my cat, but they never asked about him, we just slept a lot and ate the freezer-burnt casserole, and then I would ask for more and more and more more more blankets.

I should have realized, but they don't write columns or make books about how to make sure your boyfriend isn't dead they just call you dumb if you refuse to take notice. Maybe I'll write a column about the warning signs: the smell, the smell, check his feet, moss is okay, but mold is mold, and that is bad, the cat always knows.

Next time I will notice. I promise. Next time I will tuck you in at night and smell your feet and I will eat my meals with you, but I will not touch your sausage or your special mustard; I will only eat yellow mustard, no bun please.

The Townspeople

There is a whole world under my bed. A town with people and lovers. I try to catch peeks, sneak glimpses, steal a glance, but the world moves too fast for me to ever see.

My cat is mayor. I am not sure if there was an election or if it is a dictatorship. I think one day she found them and said, listen, and they did. I think that leaves us somewhere in between.

She won't talk to me anymore, and I think it's because she is a mayor of a town I cannot see. She thinks she's better than me. It has destroyed our relationship.

I hear the town at night, the strobe lights illuminate my bed. I can hear the cardboard houses being constructed, and within ten minutes it all seems to be built and sturdy.

I start to peek my head under sometimes, but as soon as my bed creaks you can hear the last wind, the final dust blow through like in a movie.

My cat just meows. She stares at me and meows like she isn't a mayor, like I don't know what has been happening under my bed. She meows like she is only a cat.

It scared me at first. This secret universe, this portal to a good time that hides underneath my bed. I thought that it would swallow me whole one day.

I think now that I will have to swallow it. My cat included. I wait for the daytime to leak through in their city limits so that I can construct my own town.

I cannot move under my bed with them, but perhaps in the hallway, preferably in the bathtub, a dam protecting us from utter destruction.

In my town there are only baseball fields with no houses and no referees. In my town people only eat apricots and oranges. In my town my cat is still the mayor.

She would have to accept the job; I can't picture it any other way. Her duties becoming all that she is—a workaholic.

My town closes during the nighttime, not yet fully built. People haven't moved in yet, but I've had some calls about my listings on craigslist. I'm doing tours next week.

When the moon howls I can hear my cat tell the DJ to start playing. They always sound like they're having fun, I can't help but cry.

In my town I construct treehouses where all the squirrels can live. I begin to show people the town, but there is little interest. I think I have to drop the price.

In the town under my bed there is no rent, only fun. There exist no ropes, no VIPs (besides my cat), and no more limits. The town goes on forever, slowly encroaching on the tub.

In my town I try to schmooze the people who matter, I try to build condos in their names, but I only have one taker. He tells me he doesn't want neighbors anyway.

During the day I leave flyers for my town under my bed, but by the time the people come out they have all been taken down. I think my cat has eaten them.

During the night I can hear the murmur of a riot but not of the town, only of me. They want me gone; they want to party. The bed has finally become the bathtub.

In my town, people begin to build swimming pools, and they sunbathe during the day. In my town we have a good school system but no children.

In the town under my bed the children come out as adults, adults with a drinking problem. In that town they only have time for raves.

I pretend to sleep at night, but I can feel the tiny pitchforks piercing my skin. I pretend I don't know, I pretend it doesn't bother me. I lather my wounds in Vaseline.

My cat has visited my town, but it bores her. She doesn't meow once, and I know this is a bad sign. My cat has grown tired of a world without cardboard.

In my town we have zero waste. In my town we only eat organic. In my town my cat pees on the people and laughs. She never wanted to rule.

In the town under my bed they have no limits. In that town they eat whatever they want and can stay skinny. In that town they have begun the fire.

I can feel the heat before I see the plumes of smoke. I am crying, which I hope will put out the flames. I pretend I don't notice. The dam has yet to break; they want the fire, the pain.

My cat neglects her duties of mayor in my town. The people are lost in chaos at whom to tell their problems to. They think I am the mayor, but I tell them they're mistaken.

If only my cat had realized her potential. If only she thought of what doing her taxes could do, if she thought of a future instead of her town and the cardboard.

I fear for the future of my town once the people under my bed win the fight. They are dumb people, the citizens of my town. They won't survive long; they never have.

At night I hear the towns merging. No one cared about living in a condo named after them; everyone prefers cardboard. The dam has broken, but only fun came out.

The smoke is rising, and it's hard for me to breathe. My cat has remorse, but her job as mayor must come first. She has her priorities straight.

Filing Cabinet

Filed away under:

Young Age: Eating Disorder:

    Almost Eating Disorder

        Quit Too Early

        Could Have Lasted Longer

           Never Hospitalized

           Hopeful Hospitalization

                Article: "Why Didn't I Keep Going Until it Was so Bad I Never Got my Period

Again?"

Article: "Why Didn't I Keep Going Until
I Could Never be Fat Again?"

Paragraph: Death

Filed away under:

Needy Teenage Girl: Hair Dying Techniques that Solicit Attention

Blue, Purple, Red but unnatural, Pink, Orange,

Article: Post Them all on Instagram:
#scenegirls #rad #emo #dyedhair
#diedhair #pleasepayattentiontome.

Filed away under:

Late Night Bathroom Trips: Phone Call or Cutting Myself? (This one
has trails, this one has rabbit holes, this one breeds insects.)

Listen to the Door, Sad Music Means Happy, Happy Music
Means Blood

Article: "Why Every Teenager Learns How to Pick Locks"

Filed away under:

Summoning Demons: Thinking You're More Magical Than You Are.

Filed away under:

Acrylic Nails: Asking for Cancer Risks.

Filed away under:

Positive Affirmations: People Like You, People Like You, People Like

You, People *most likely* Like You.

Filed away under:

Realism: Most People Most Likely Do Not Know You Exist

    That is Why You Must Dye Your Hair

        Article: Instagram logistics: #payattentiontome.

Filed away under:

Parents.

    Mom and Dad.

        Article: "Being the Middle Child Sucks."

        Cross-reference with "Being the Oldest Sucks"
        and "Being the Youngest Sucks."

Filed away under:

Music: Good Music Makes You *Feel* Something.

    But Only What I Consider Feelings.

    Subsections: Punk, Pop Punk, Pop Alt, Emo, Rock, Alt Rock,
    Prog Pop Punk.

        Article: "Why You Can Never
        Recreate Punk Music Anymore,"
        Paragraph: "What Even is a Genre
        Anyway?"

        Sentence: "I *Feel* It."

Filed away under:

Possible Careers With a Future: surgeon, teacher, bank robber, lawyer, diplomat, porn star, star star, Guinness World Record holder, alcoholic, leech, sugar baby, model, psychologist, doctor.

Filed away under:

My Career Path: writer.

Filed away under:

Wishing to Be a Witch: me, with my dad's permission.

When I was Little I Could Disappear

Article: "Or at Least That's What They Said,"

Paragraph: "Maybe They Just Wanted to Get Rid of Me."

Filed away under:

Fiancé: Tall, Handsome, Skinny: Too Skinny

Humor: Dry

Hair: Dry

Dandruff: Green

Bonuses: Funny, Non-romantic, Likes Chipotle, Tall

Filed away under:

Self-categorization: Needy, Vulnerable: Needy, Living: Dead, Dramatic, Positive, #payattentiontome

Filed away under Accomplishments: .

Filed away under:

Household: Every Room Is White, My Eyeballs Radiate Whiteness

The Light at Night Is Bright; Even the Darkness is White.

Filed away:

My Home

Subsection: My Ghosts

The Ending

I don't finish books. They're a waste of time. They go on so that you can sit on the edge, waiting for the tectonic plates to shift so that you're thrown off. The endings lead to nowhere. They lead to cul-de-sacs of thought, and no one wants to live in a circle.

I don't finish words because everyone already guesses what word I'm saying. If I break someone's heart saying the wrong word, then their heart is still broken.

I thought about dying, about killing myself, joining others, but even this ending isn't an ending, it's only the beginning of a different end in a different circle that exists just as much as this one does.

I saw an ending once, but it's still alive inside my mind. I still dream of them and yell at them. We still converse. They might think they're dead, but their ending only began my dreams.

I think she ended it for me. I think she ended herself in exchange for a curse that makes me hungry. I'm the only one who feels cursed. She won't let me forget it; I can't stop the hunger. I can't stop eating. There are no more sacrifices to be made.

I ended a relationship, I've ended many, but none of them stop existing. They linger, lost, looming over me, waiting for me to forget and die so that they can mourn someone they only pretend to know.

I ended a life: that wasn't a murder but just a fight. Words can end what they began, and when they start, the ending is never good.

I don't think anything is ever over. I don't think you should read on. This is the ending. Here. Now. Stop reading.

My Haunted Home

My haunted home is filling with fog. Inside this home, this haunted home, it is becoming foggy, hazy, hard to see, hard to breathe through the people, the grey, the hazy hazy haze. In this haunted home I can't walk without bumping into someone in the foggy traffic, but they're all just dust, so the bump is more of a gag, a cough, a hacking of a lung because I can't breathe through them.

My mother moved in first. She killed herself years ago. She appeared in my bathroom, she seeped out of my fingernails, she birthed herself from my womb. I held her inside of me since the years of her death, and she emerged without hesitation, no C-section, natural and raw. I'm not sure how she found me. I moved away, ran across state lines like a fugitive, but she could smell my baby breath and my fearful tears from miles away.

My mother acted like I needed her, like I wished her into this existence, but I don't remember those feelings of mourning. It felt like the old times for a while. It felt like when I was younger, and her back wasn't broken. It felt like how it is supposed to feel—like your mom is alive and whole, not crushed into ash in your living room.

I think for a while this reality felt right. It felt like I was Baby, and she was Mother. I couldn't remember the time when I had birthed her. I only remembered the times when she carried me into bed from the car when my legs wanted to sleep. It felt like kisses from your parents on the tip of a cut—life had been alleviated.

It felt far too soon, but my aunt moved in after her—sisters have to stick together. I asked for her to pitch in, pay rent, kiss the tips of my paper cuts, but she was too busy. She killed herself years ago. Too, she killed herself years ago too. Because of this she was too busy reassembling her broken body, sprawled out on the asphalt, she collected herself in bags and tried to put together her own puzzle.

I blame my mother. She must have lit a match, and, like moths, like mosquitoes, like bears and bugs and evil things, they came.

I don't think they're evil, but they take up too much room. They sit on the couch eating their coffee cake and they never clean up their crumbs.

My grandpa—their father—followed, keeping the family together. He was murdered years ago. Or so they say, but in my haunted home rumors are a reality because they're dead anyway. He likes to sit next to me on the couch but never leaves enough room. He reminds me of days of sugar and days of candy. He is, he was, he pretends to still be a toothache waiting to happen.

My boyfriend was next, but he is alive. He's been alive for years now. Now I sit wedged between my boyfriend and my grandfather. My mother and her sister are making dinner in the kitchen, but they won't share because they won't make enough. They say they are only able to feed people who kill themselves. My boyfriend isn't aware. He thinks I like to sit close and just asks what that smell is. The smell is always a haunting.

His uncle was next. He died in a hospital years ago. He is far too mature to live in this house, at least peacefully. He doesn't get along with my mother. He likes to drink, and she likes to pick arguments. Don't waste your liver, she says. I'm already dead, he says. She tried to hit him with an umbrella, but ghosts don't have umbrellas to hit with. She always forgets this.

His grandfather followed. He lived too long, he died too short, years ago. He speaks too fast for anyone to listen, but I think my boyfriend can hear him. I see his ears wiggle when they get close, unsure, unwilling, but still at ease. It has always been his tell, the ears of someone who wishes they could hear more than they do.

My great-grandmother and her daughter came together. They came and sat, their knees intact, their arms by their sides, and their teeth glued in. They died years apart, years ago. I always knew she was waiting, my great-grandmother. She always had a soft spot for her daughter. Their wrinkles have smoothed, and their hair has thickened, but the way that they smell remains: remnants of smoke and shit. I wouldn't want it any other way.

My uncle took longer to get here, although I'm sure he was the first to die. He killed himself years ago. Or so they say. The drugs or the train, we're not sure. I'm happy he came; death looks better on him than life ever did.

It only took days after for my other uncle to come. It seems as though drugs live in the family, in the veins of their needle lives, ready to hurt those around them. I think, though, they missed each other. I think, mostly, they wish they had been able to go together.

My boyfriend's grandmother came with her husband. Both had died in different years, but those years seem as though they are the same by now. They don't like anyone else here, and I don't blame them. They gossip in the corner and pretend they do not. I don't think they particularly care to be called back into this house, not with those they had wanted to leave.

My haunted home is becoming crowded. I expected three at most, but the fog is so thick that my boyfriend can't see anymore. He won't ask the question because he knows the answer. He knows the dead people are here, he knows his grandfather won't stop talking, he knows my mom tried to beat his uncle, and he knows the elbows are too close to separate at this point.

My alive boyfriend is moving out because this was never his home. He moved in too late to unpack his bags. All the shelves were taken, all the drawers were stuffed, and all the hangers had been hung.

My dead mother is mad at him. Mad at me for letting him move out. I want to move out too, but I'm afraid she'll try to hit me with the umbrella she doesn't have. I'm afraid to lose the magical kisses of a mother to a daughter, but the truth is that she has become too busy with hosting duties to cure my pain.

My alive boyfriend calls to me from beyond. From beyond my haunted home that I love so much. He calls to me to bring my bags; he's bringing me with. This was never my home, and he knows it. I just needed a place to crash. I just missed living with my mom. I just wanted to have a family again. He calls to me from beyond the fog, from beyond the greys and the haze. He calls to me, and I have to squint past his grandparents fucking, past the wrinkles that have left.

My neighbors have died and moved in. My mom is in love again. In love with hosting, saving a spot for my dad when he decides to join. My mom is wishing now she had accepted the empty nest.

My mom has told me I need to grow up. My mom told me that my boyfriend is right: what kind of twenty-two-year old lives with her dead mom? Grow up, grow out.

My haunted home is gone. It has become alive with the smell of death, with the emptiness of fog, full of the absence of umbrellas.

My haunted home was never my own.

PART II

You, Your Fault

You wake up in the morning thinking that you know your left from your right. That you know which way you have to take to work. You're falling into a routine. This routine is simple because you may only know simplicity. You may only know the things you have always been accustomed to. Slowly becoming accustomed to more, to slight changes, to things that always felt so familiar that you don't realize they're different.

You wake up in the morning and roll out of bed to your left. You place your feet on the floor. The floor is sturdy. You feel sturdy. You make a pot of black tea because you heard from a friend that coffee is like crack, and your sister is a crackhead, and you don't want to defend her any longer. You drink your tea after it rests for twenty minutes. You like it black. Black, black tea. Your throat lubricates itself, the warm liquids becoming your liquids, you mixing yourself into the teacup, you becoming the sugar, the milk, you becoming the sweetness, the hotness, the cool melody of black tea. Black, black tea.

You work from home most of the time. You still get dressed as though people will see you. You put on clothes that didn't cost much, but you feel like they were a fortune. You feel that they look like they look like they cost a fortune. They look mediocre. You do not put on shoes or socks. You paint your toenails. You sit at your desk. You take a lunch break from 11:15 a.m. until noon. Then you clock out at 4 p.m. You smile every time you clock out because you even bought one of those vintage timekeeper clocks, and you keep a punch card there. The first time you used it you cut yourself open, and the jam inside your body leaked and spilled and marinated into the rust. You got a tetanus shot.

Usually for dinner you would make chicken or salmon. Tonight we are having chicken. You bake it in the oven with potatoes and green beans. You make yourself think it was from the farmers' market and not just the grocery store, but there isn't a farmers' market close enough because you ride a bike. A bike that might also give you tetanus.

You eat your dinner and watch TV. Usually you will watch something funny but not animated. Tonight you watch a drama. You think about the time you lived with roommates and you could watch a horror movie, but you are too scared. You will cry. You will conjure something greater than you. You turn off the drama and turn on a comedy because you've already scared yourself. You go to bed at 9 p.m. Before bed you pee, but you also convince yourself you have to pee even more, so for an hour or so you go back and pee seven more times because you don't want to be woken up at 4 a.m. to pee. So you pee once more.

Then you go to bed.

You had always convinced yourself that locks on the door made you safe and that neighbors meant people would never see you. You were always paranoid. You still are. You are used to people dying, which makes you feel like you're also already almost entirely dead. You're not sure if it bothers you.

Inside your apartment are two bedrooms, one for work and one for sleeping. A small kitchen in which you sit when you're not working. One bathroom with a tub-shower. You prefer showers because tubs are intimate and vulnerable. You have flowers in every room besides your sleeping room. You have allergies. You own fourteen candles, but there are only two out—bathroom and kitchen. Your walls are a mix of white, beige, and blue. Your sheets are cheap and soft in the way you hope cheap sheets will be. You sleep at night with a nightguard. You usually wake up scared.

When you were twelve you told your parents that you wanted to be abducted by aliens, and they told you that if you want it, they won't take you. You spent months marching outside of your house with picket signs that read: **I hate aliens, I don't want to ever be abducted by aliens, I love my family**. Your parents thought it was funny until one night you ran away into the backyard because your friend at school who did get abducted said you have to be outside in trees when it happens. It took your parents three hours to find you, and when you saw the flashing blue lights you thought it was time; you thought you had finally done it. You've never gotten any closer since.

Now in your room under your bed you hide the signs that you made when you were younger. When you go to family reunions they make fun of you. They think it was all fun and games, but really you never lost the hope to be special. You're not sure what could be more special than being chosen out of all humans to fly into space with beings you didn't know. You have a list of questions prepared; you'd want to become one of them. You'd never want to go home. You would have a family. A new family. Sadly, you aren't allowed to go. They'll never choose you, but you will send them mail like little kids send Santa lists.

Your mom comes over unannounced every Thursday with soup that you don't eat because you hate soup. She knows you hate soup, but she is trying to convince you otherwise. You think she hates you.

One day you decide to ask her why she always brings you soup. "It's good for the skin," she says. "You look a little dry. Worn down. I'm trying to plump those cheeks back to when you were a baby so you can give me babies."

"I don't want babies."

"Every girl wants babies."

You eat your soup because you're sure that mother must know best. You're sure one day you will want babies even though you know you don't want babies. You tell yourself that when you have the babies you don't want that you'll never force them to eat soup. You plan to have them the same day your mother dies so she never even gets to meet them. You'll tell her on her deathbed that you're pregnant, and she'll try to hold on just long enough to meet the babies she always wanted you to want, but you will hold out just a little longer. You'll never say goodbye. They will never eat soup.

When she leaves you throw out the remaining soup. Even the drain hates that they have to eat it, and you hear it gurgle and murmur and complain.

You weren't always so angry. You weren't always a sad sack that had been left in the rain. You used to be an umbrella. You used to be colorful and full of life. There was a time when you were perfect, when your life was perfect. You only know this from the disappointment you face now.

In this time, way back when, you never skinned your knees. You always flew off the swing and onto the mulch of the playground. During this time you could feel air on your teeth and not cringe from the cold. There was a time when you could sit down at dinner and eat every last drop—sometimes seconds, sometimes thirds, sometimes the table and the chairs and your family and friends. There was a time when you would pick flowers on the road with your friends. During this time you never knew that kids could die, that people could become earth, that the ground was made up of as many dead things as you are now. There was a time in life when you had friends who were alive, who wouldn't die. You remember your first kiss against the soft, gentle lips and the mysterious giggles that sank beneath them. There was a time when a kiss wasn't a cruel dare but only a show of affection. There was a time when you felt warmth under the hands of others, not just stone logs that fell on top of you.

During this time of happiness, you felt whole. You didn't know it then, but when bugs are only an inconvenience and not a fixture in your house that you're too afraid to confront, it becomes clear. You used to be a whole human, you used to be long and free and sway in the wind like a flag, but you have melted into a puddle that your mother has turned into soup.

The weekends are your favorite because sometimes you go on dates or see your neighbor Emily and her husband, John, whom you have a crush on. She doesn't know this because wives never like to know, neither do husbands. Usually no one cares about your thoughts.

This weekend you go to the carnival that is in town on a second date with a girl you thought looked better in her pictures. You don't tell her this because you think it would upset her, but you think she knows; you can tell by how she walks. She holds your hand, you hold hers, and you share funnel cake together even though you're trying to lose weight. In the moments that you lick the sugar off her fingers you feel like you weigh the right amount, like you might be weightless, like you could float above everyone.

You're never quite sure how to invite someone inside your house, so you linger by your doorstep until you've been outside for twenty minutes. You blurt out, "Come upstairs," and this sentence ends in both a question mark and an exclamation point, maybe even in a whisper. She follows you, and you can feel the wind stay trapped outside. You try to convince yourself that she isn't there to murder you or punish you or sacrifice you to some god. You ask her, "Are you going to murder me?" She tells you no.

"Would you tell me the truth if you were going to?"

"Probably not, but I haven't lied to anyone about it yet." You trust her. You undress her. She undresses you, and soon you are two dirty, lumpy sacks of filth and scum lying on top of each other between pools of sweat and breath.

"Are you an alien?" you ask her, wishing, dreaming, remembering not to want it too bad, feeling the throbbing of the sign under your bed.

She laughs. "Not that I know of."

"Would you tell me the truth if you were?"

"I'd be more likely to tell you that than if I were going to murder you."
She smiles, and you smile, but inside all you can picture is the knife she
must be holding behind her back. You run to the bathroom.

"I'll be right back," you shout from inside and you can hear her scurry
to the door.

"Do you want me to be an alien? I mean I guess I could."

"No, no, I just have to pee. I always do. It's not healthy. I should go to
the doctor." You can feel that she is disgusted and disturbed and you
don't know why you ever invited her up here. She isn't a murderer, but
she isn't an alien, and you should be holding out for one or the other.
You exit the bathroom. She is naked in your bed, and you picture what
it would be like if she were real and physical and could give you the
babies your mom wants but you never want but you might want if your
mom is right. You wish there was an easy time to ask her about marriage
and adoption and all the taxes and paperwork that come with. You dig
around under your bed and pull out the signs you made when you were
younger: **I hate aliens, I don't want to ever be abducted by aliens, I
love my family**. She reads them out loud to you and when she reads
them she almost sounds like she could be calling someone to come and
steal you away with her. "Did you make these recently?"

"No, they're from when I was younger."

"I used to want to be abducted too. Not by aliens but maybe by my aunt
or uncle."

You have the urge to rip the signs up and burn them. Maybe burn it all
down. The signs and her body and yourself. Arson has always intrigued
you, but jail has always deterred you. "Would you ever commit arson?"
You ask her, but her face doesn't look at you.

"I did when I was younger. It was fun. I went to therapy, and they told me it wasn't fun, but I remember it being fun." She smirks in a way that makes it seem like it could all be a lie.

"Would you lie to me about committing arson?"

"I'd be less likely to be a murderer or an alien than an arsonist." It makes sense. You lie down in bed with her and you feel your bodies molding into one pile, one person, one object that is neither human nor physical nor tangible. You are floating in that cloud again. In the morning you wake up, still in a pile of bones and skin with her, you share coffee and she leaves. You fear she will never call you again. You throw your phone into the river.

On your walk home you remember the time that you came home and found out that your father had died. Your mother told you it wasn't your fault in a way that made it seem like it was. If it wasn't your fault then your mother never would have said it wasn't. Why would it be? Why would she put that in your head, in the universe of your body, in the same galaxy as you? In a world where cars and people kill other cars and people, there is the possibility in which you caused an accident while being at school. In this world you could be a witch or a psychic. Or even just yourself. In this world you are trapped in the guilt of all the cars and people dying. It is all your fault. All your fault. You did this to them. To all of them.

You begin to walk faster. You start jogging. You tear up and think about the time when your crackhead sister drove you to dance practice and killed a dog and their owner. The dog was a labradoodle, and the owner was a man. You think about the way your sister never got arrested, never was found, just seemed to have died somewhere in a crack alley like all the other crackheads who kill people by accident on purpose. You think about how you never made it to dance practice. If maybe you made it to dance practice then you would be a dancer now and not working from home most of the time. You think about how if you made it to dance practice you could have saved your sister, you could have saved your dad, you could have saved your friend when you were younger, you could have dismantled the whole automobile industry, you could have been a nice witch, seen the good, but instead you are a murderer. Maybe, just maybe, if you made it to dance practice you could have been abducted by aliens, maybe they were waiting there for you.

Soon you're back at your apartment, but the noises in your head don't stop. They never seem to stop. If they stopped that is how you knew you would die. Instead, you go to grab your phone to call your mom to ask for more soup, but you remember you threw it away because you were afraid some girl wouldn't call you. You go to your room and find the pay-as-you-go phone that you always keep for times that you throw your phone into the lake because you're afraid some girl won't call you. You spend about an hour setting it up, and by the time you do, you have the same number, no contacts, and receive a text from the girl you thought would never respond. You smile.

You always feel like you waste your weekends, and your mother would probably say you do. All you do is cut your toenails and fingernails and eat at restaurants that are too expensive with almost strangers. You worry you spend too much time with almost strangers, so this weekend you go to dinner with Emily and her husband, John. They are mostly boring, but you always hope they will ask you for a threesome, so you do not mind. Mostly, you daydream through dinner. You wander around in your own thoughts of what you wish you were saying and they were saying. You wish they would rip away at your dress in public, you wish they would slither up your thighs and into your undercarriage as if you were nothing but a car or a piece of meat. You dream that you could feel their air—hot, steaming wetness encompass you. You seem to melt in your seat while staring blankly at them, listening about how they are thinking of having kids, how they might have to move, oh how they wish you could go with them, how they love living next to you, how they always appreciate the soup your mother drops off for them, how they'll make the same recipe for their kids they may or may not have. You feel yourself on the edge of death from boredom at the reality of who they are.

That night you go home and call the girl you like, the possible arsonist. She comes over, and you tell her all about the threesome you wish you could have with your neighbors. You tell her that you think if you have to choose, he would be the alien, and she would be the murderer. She tells you that she will always be the arsonist. You dream of fucking her. Of crawling around in her insides, making soup out of her body, hiding her remains in bags of potatoes at the grocery store, but instead you lie next to her.

"My sister is a crackhead."

"I never tried crack."

"Me either."

"I would if someone asked me to, but I try not to hang out with crackheads."

"You could hang out with my sister."

"I think I like you more."

"She might be dead anyway. A lot of crackheads die in alleys that no one knows about."

"I think that's how Amy Winehouse would have went."

"I think that's how most people want to go."

"I'd rather go out in a car accident."

"Sometimes I cause car accidents. I might be a witch. Maybe a ghost. Maybe a god."

"Either would be cool."

You fall asleep by her feet as you watch *Ghostbusters*. You felt relaxed until you remembered that she will die in a car accident. You remember and start to cry, start to pound the walls of your dream trying to get you. You can see it happening. You can see her under the tires of the car of someone who isn't even a crackhead. You think about the pain of her bones crunching. You think about her spine becoming dislodged, part of her torn away from the rest. You picture her as a rack of ribs seasoned with asphalt. It is as if you have carved her own casket, like you dug her grave. You begin to cry, and she wakes you up. You ask her to move in, and she laughs. You tell her your dream, her reality. She says, "At least it's a self-fulfilling prophecy."

She leaves in the morning, and all day you watch the news, waiting to hear about her death. About the pile up on I-95, about the little kid who saw her body and will go on to shoot up a school, about her ghost who flew out of her and into an evil grandma, about the arsonist streak going around the city. You sit and watch for a week straight. You do not remember sleeping, but you know you must have. On Sunday you hear a knock on your door, and it is her. "I guess you're not a witch after all."

You crawl inside of her skin. You dismantle, disassemble, desecrate her skin and bones and the fragile veins and vessels inside her. You

127

open her up and clear out her insides; you set up shop and zip her up. You wear her like a suit or like a briefcase. You move into her fingers and toes and you stretch her skin until it fits you like a sock. Then you lay next to her, both of you panting, both of you glowing. "I should not die more often." You both laugh.

You've been dating for six months now, and she asks when she can meet your mom. You tell her your mom has never met any of your girlfriends, only boyfriends. She repeats her question. You tell her that your mom stops by unannounced every Thursday with soup. She tells you she hates soup; you tell her you hate soup.

On Thursday she comes over, and so does your mom. "Mom, this is my girlfriend."

"Oh when I was your age I had so many girlfriends. We used to have slumber parties and get-togethers. It's so nice to meet you, sweetie." For about twenty minutes you all eat soup in silence, only your mother is the only one actually eating soup. You and your girlfriend are throwing it on the floor and in plants and at each other. Your mom pretends not to notice.

At the end of soup you decide that now seems as good a time as any, so you get down on one knee and propose to your girlfriend. "You set me on fire. Marry me?"

She says yes. Your mom leaves. In a few days you get a congratulations card in the mail from your mom. She wrote, "Lesbians can still have babies." When she comes over with soup the next time, she has brought multiple books and pamphlets about baby care and baby names and how to find a surrogate and where to find a donor and also a gift card to Babies "R" Us (also good at Toys "R" Us).

When your mom leaves, your girlfriend moves in. Sorry, your fiancée the arsonist moves in. You tell her that you also want to be an arsonist because you can't be a murderer or an alien. She tells you that you could be anything. You smile. One night you tell her that you've always wanted to be a cult leader or maybe just a cult member. You tell her you've always wanted to be a part of something bigger. You spend the rest of the night watching documentaries about Jonestown. "He's too obvious," she tells you. She's right.

You wake up in the morning and realize your whole routine has changed without telling you because now you get up and get out of bed on the right side because she likes the left. You realize that now you take an hour for lunch instead of forty-five minutes. You forget to clock out on your old tetanus machine and you haven't ridden your bike in a month because she has a car. You never get in the car, but you decide to walk. One day at breakfast you start crying. You tell her that you've never had tetanus, you can't plan a wedding, and she never taught you how to be an arsonist. You begin crying harder, and she lays you down on the bed and dresses you like a baby. Like the baby you don't want but think you might want if your mother is correct. After you're dressed she takes you by the hand and walks you down to an alley about half a mile away. She has gasoline and a match in her pocket. She gives you gloves.

"Don't forget to wipe everything off before you throw it. Aim carefully. Don't run away from the fire. Don't call 911. Start screaming right away. Get someone else's attention and start crying. Make them call. Aim carefully."

You douse the alley and the cardboard in gasoline and you throw a match at it. The match goes out before it lights it. "Sometimes you have to try again." She reaches in her pocket and passes you another. You try seventeen times before it works. It seems like it is all at once. Like one second there is silence and cold, damp air; the next you are filled with anger, with flames, with the likelihood of death. You start to cry. You run away. You get someone's attention, and they call 911. You are gone and home before the sirens begin. You close your eyes and picture the ash and the heat. You feel like you are an oven, like you are a chef, like you are the start of the world. You smile. On the news you learn that three crackheads died in the fire, only they don't call them crackheads, but you know that they are. "I am a witch," you tell your fiancée. "No, you're an arsonist," she tells you.

Sometimes when she fucks you, you feel like burning her down. You think about what it would be like to call her a crackhead, to give her a name, for her to be your sister and to burn her until she is as crisp as crostini. It makes you scream.

"I think I want more than anything to be an alien."

"That is the hardest one to be."

"No, a cult leader is. I'm not very outgoing."

"True, but you can't wish to be abducted. It just happens."

You start crying when she tells you this because it's true and you know it. You hate her just as much as you hate your mom in this moment. You yell at her. She told you, before, that you could be anything you wanted. She let you be. She made you feel like it was possible. "You helped me be an arsonist. You helped me fulfill my dreams."

She starts crying now because she thought that would be enough. She thought if she could give you something it would be better than to give you nothing. "I even helped you be a murderer. Why can't those be enough? I'll join your cult. I will abduct you."

"You don't understand." You yell this at her again and again until you feel her beating you. You feel her ghosts leaving her; you want to help her understand. "You don't understand. I want to be gone: I want to be above with them."

This is when she seems to understand. This is when you know she understands you because you can see the flames in her eyes like when she helped you burn down the crackheads.

She leaves and comes back, and soon you are both doing crack. "I don't even drink coffee."

"Coffee is worse than crack." She tells you this, and you know it's true. "When it starts, imagine that you are being abducted."

You smoke the crack and soon you can picture the UFO coming to get you. You no longer feel like a witch or a psychic, but you feel like something else. Someone else. You feel like your skin is becoming rubber, like you are turning into a different species. You feel like there could never be any more car accidents, not when you are with them. Above Earth, there are no more cars. You feel yourself smiling, but your skin is not your own. It is the skin of a thousand creatures turned into one. The feeling is like a hairless cat with hair, but not the right hair, not cat hair, not human, but rubber hair that doesn't exist. You feel more connected now than ever to your fiancée, the arsonist, the murderer, the alien. You feel like you are one.

The next morning you both skip work to do more crack. One more time, you tell each other, that's what they always say. Only this time you were right. You only did crack one more time and this time you were not a rubbery alien but sadly just a regular hairless cat that everyone thought was ugly. You throw the rest of the crack into the lake.

At your wedding you say in your vows that she makes you fly higher than a UFO, and no one laughs besides you two. In attendance at the wedding are your mom, Emily and her husband, John, a minister of the peace, and your fiancée's, sorry, wife's brother, Ulysses. Everyone cries.

At the end of the wedding everyone goes home, and you go back to your apartment with your wife and you fuck her as if she is a stranger again. As if you were aliens. As if you were cannibals and you had a never-ending supply of meat. You fuck her so hard that you bash her head in and she dies, but only in metaphor. In reality you are both happy.

In a few days you get a card from your mother who has stopped coming over unannounced on Thursday that says, "Lesbians can have babies too!" You feel like you're stuck in a time loop. You feel like nothing is real anymore. Like love is only a creation, a word that means nothing, a manifestation of this unassuming need to procreate. You tell your wife. "Let's kill your mother." You tell her you don't like the idea. "Let's kill ourselves." You tell her you don't like the idea. "Let's kill your neighbors." You tell her you don't like the idea. "Let's kill Ulysses." She tells you she doesn't like the idea. You go to sleep.

You decide you still don't want kids. At least not now or ever and especially if soup is still in existence. You tell her instead that you'd rather burn down an orphanage. She tells you that's too high profile. You ask if maybe you could on your anniversary. She says maybe. Rather, though, maybe you'll eat them.

Acknowledgments

Thank you to *Interpret* magazine for being the first to publish "The Lemons, Mmm" and supporting my writing. Thank you to *pioneertown* and Brenna Kischuk for giving "Charles" a home and believing in my writing.

Thank you to everyone at FC2 and the University of Alabama Press for all your support throughout this process. I could not have done it without you. Thank you to Vi Khi Nao for choosing *My Haunted Home* as the winner of the Ronald Sukenick Innovative Fiction Contest—you truly made my dreams come true.

This book would not have happened without my parents. Mom, I miss you every day. Though this book is filled with grief and mourning and all the thoughts that haunt me, though this book could not have happened without you always telling me to keep writing, though this book is due to not having you around, I would trade all of it to have you back. Dad, you inspire me. I grew up watching you write, watching you read, and wanting to be just like you. Well, I guess I won—where's your book, huh? I love you always, Dad. You made me me.

To my siblings who very much don't love my writing—at least some people do! Emma, you are my best friend, one of my favorite editors, and also the coolest, funniest person I know. Tyler, you taught me how to mosh, how to crowd-surf—basically all my street cred is because of you.

To my husband who watched me edit this book the same summer we got married and moved—thanks for dealing with me. Harry, you bring life to my writing. I strive to impress you just like you always impress me. This book would not be complete without your constant support and feedback. The best editor is the songwriter. Thank you for making space for me.

Thank you, Skitty: you are the cat of my dreams (and my nightmares). You inspired so many of these stories, and I could not have done it without your endless starring and fuzzy cuddles.

Thank you to Greg Howard who helped shape my writing in a time that helped me define what I wanted to do. Thank you, Greg, for always reading about my dead mom.

Thank you to Hollie Adams who helped me revise many of these stories and allowed me a place in her workshop that felt like home.

Thank you to the University of Maine English Department and the amazing faculty who continuously support their students. You gave me the home that let me create.

Thank you to all my friends who have workshopped with me (both formally and informally), the friends who supported me even though they don't like horror, the friends who just listened when I needed to talk. Thank you, Amber, Erin, Kaitlyn, Kyle, Lydia, Martin, Morghen.

Thank you to my family who have also been waiting for this moment with me: Little Grandma, Aunt Marie, Grandpa Joe, Nana Susan, Bethanne, and my beautiful sister-in-law, Kate.

Thank you to the bands McCafferty and The Tenth for being on loop in my brain, in my heart, and on my Alexa as I wrote and rewrote this book.

Thank you to whoever took the time to read this. I love you more than you know.